The Years Twitch

A Novel

By Kristian Dunn

Copyright © 2016 Kristian Dunn

All rights reserved.

ISBN-13: 978-1537139852
ISBN-10: 1537139851

Thanks to: India Dunn, George Dunn, Danya Shegoleff, Ron Fleming, Jim Devers, Martha Conway, Jimmy Jazz, Frances McMaster, Matt Dunn and Murali Sastry

1.

William Olson's back was aching. The knotted tree roots on which he sat made his butt fall asleep. This old, hard tree was not fond of strangers. At least that was how he imagined this conifer: a pissed-off tree.

The other three American soldiers there with him, Special Ops, to be specific, didn't seem to mind the cold Afghan night and the lack of convenience. Their eyes were trained, seemingly without distraction, on a small one-story building erected on the valley floor fifty yards below. William figured this ability to concentrate was one among many traits that separated him, a recent addition to Special Forces, who was chosen for this mission mainly because of his ability to speak Pashto, from these experienced warriors.

With his night-vision goggles cinched down tightly on his face, he looked down at the dozen or so mud based buildings waiting forebodingly on valley floor below. It was late, probably midnight, and every home was dark with the exception of this one. Through one of the windows, which was covered with a cloth, shadows of the inhabitants would come and go. There had to be a small fire inside. The men's silhouettes created a glowing, fuzzy, fiction of life. It was hard to tell how many were inside. William guessed four.

For a moment he considered his aching body. His head hurt because of his helmet and his nvgs and his shoulders were in pain because of the heavy gear he'd been carrying for miles over rough terrain. In this exhausted state he was expected to make life or death decisions. His gut tightened.

Just as William was about to allow himself some self pity, JP, one of the Special Ops guys, said quietly into his commlink, "Moving out." William's pulse instantly started pounding as the command made its way through his communication system into the tiny speaker squeezed into his left ear.

The mountains in this part of Afghanistan thrust into the air as if they were trying to punch the sky. They were tall, powerful and threatening. William thought they almost looked out of place, as if they'd been pulled from Colorado and dropped into the middle of the desert. Enough snow was scattered across the top of them that they looked like a ski resort could own them. These were angry mountains.

As his anxiety grew, he kept reminding himself that he had killed before, or at least he thought he had. When firing from a long distance at multiple targets with several other American soldiers firing as well… it was just hard to tell. The agitation of the thoughtful side of his mind versus the obstinate, disciplined side had thus far been bearable. In a way, he didn't really want to know if he had killed.

His platoon was charged with establishing and maintaining a forward post. It was the furthest US post north of the main local Marine base, and it was a two-hour foot patrol away. They had been successful, but every day they were attacked at least once and after the battle their enemies would disappear into the wilderness. After a week of this, he got word that he would be leaving the next day.

Drone flights and satellite intelligence had discovered this building. It was thought that the Taliban had established some sort of headquarters here after stealing it from its rightful owners. Probably the orders to attack the American base had originated here. One young man, apparently in his twenties, seemed to always be in or near the building. His only identifiable characteristics that differentiated him from the others who came and went were a large scar on his right cheek and his small stature. He looked to be less than five foot five; and he was the Special Ops' target. If he was the mastermind behind the Taliban's movements in this area, William's commanders wanted to "have a chat with him." Those were the actual words they used. This one was to be brought back down the mountain alive if possible. The others were expected to be dispatched.

Inside the building frustration mingled with boredom and weariness. Miftah, the aforementioned short young man with a scar, his father, Abdul-Baari and two others sat around the small fire.

"I'm cold and uncomfortable," sighed Abdul-Baari in Pashto. Miftah was crouched down, holding his hands out in front of the flames, trying to stay warm. The other two sat on the ground, crossed legged with AK-47 assault rifles across their laps and small teacups in their hands. Miftah looked at them and smiled slightly at the absurdity.

"They are hours late, this is ridiculous," Abdul-Baari barked.

"They'll be here," Miftah replied.

Abdul-Baari stared at him for a moment then looked away. "If they're alive," he muttered.

It was slow going descending the hill above the valley. William and the other three soldiers didn't want their targets to hear them coming so they positioned themselves downwind. Even with that advantage, a small twig cracking under his foot could easily be heard dozens of yards away. He was thankful the targets in the inside were burning a fire. That little fire would help conceal their approach and could help control the outcome of the fight that he was sure awaited them. After a few moments he reached another tree and positioned himself against it so that he could use it for cover but still see the building.

The Years Twitch

―――――――

Miftah felt the hairs on the back of his neck rise up. He looked up and towards the door, which was slightly ajar.

"What is it?" Abdul-Baari asked.

"Shhh!" Miftah hissed back at him. Abdul-Baari's eyebrows rose in surprise to this disrespect. And just as fast as they rose, they descended, pointing towards his nose, not happy with this youngster's attitude.

Miftah raised is hands in front of him and bowed his head slightly, as if to silently say, "I'm sorry, bear with me."

"Hmmff," Abdul-Baari responded.

Crack.

All four of them heard it and snapped their heads towards the door. Somebody outside had stepped on a twig in the distance. Anxiously one of the men stood, ran to the entrance and pointed his rifle through the space between the door and the doorjamb. He then peered out a little further. There were a couple of more snaps and the clear sound of footsteps rapidly approaching. There was more than one person coming.

―――――――

The Special Ops were within fifty feet of the building, slowly making their way. William's mouth was remarkably dry and he could feel his heart beating in his ears. What reaction would their arrival bring? He unlocked the safety on his M4 rifle and pointed it forward. His job was to stay outside and pick off anyone trying to escape. Pushing himself against a tree for support, he prepared to fire.

The sounds of the footsteps outside of the building were getting closer. Miftah held his breath. The others were nervous, too. One of the men dropped his teacup on the floor and stood up, pointing his machine gun at the entrance. He waited for a moment and then uttered the Pashto equivalent of "fuck this" and charged out.

"No, wait!" Miftah yelled.

It was too late; he was gone. Abdul-Baari and Miftah looked at each other, worried.

William's focus was abruptly distracted when he heard loud, running footsteps nearby. They were ahead of him and to his right, coming from beyond the tree line. He froze. In his peripheral vision he saw that the other special ops guys were frozen, too. He was unsure of what to do. Only about ten yards ahead of him two men in local Afghan dress with machine guns slung over their shoulders popped out from the trees and ran past him down a path towards the small village. Apparently William hadn't been seen.

The door of the home flew open and a tall man with an AK-47 rifle ran out.

"Who's there?" he yelled in Pashto as he pointed his gun towards the runners.

"It's Mohammad!" the lead runner yelled back.

"Ah," he sighed and pointed his gun toward the sky. Once the runners reached him, the three men greeted and embraced. William could no longer make out what they were saying, but the two runners were out of breath and clearly relieved. Chatting and laughing, two of them headed into the home, but one remained outside. Still panting from his run, he looked over his shoulder. William could have sworn the man looked right at him. But he turned his glance past William's position and continued to scan the area. William thought he could somehow sense the intruders' presence. The man's head stopped turning when his line of sight reached JP's position. William could see the man squint while moving his face slightly forward, struggling to see what was out in the dark tree line.

From the inside came the voices of all the men, greeting each other and chatting. They didn't notice that one of their party hadn't yet come in.

The man pulled his machine gun off of his shoulder, pointed it towards JP and took a tentative step forward. He was unsure whether or not there was a real threat out there, but he was clearly going to investigate.

The four American soldiers had taken positions behind trees, carbine rifles pointed forward. William felt that the blanket of black above seemed to push down on them through the trees with some sort of disinterested brawn.

JP's arm slowly rose, fell and moved left and right following the advancing man's moving head. Letting out a slow breath, JP squeezed his trigger.

Click! Click!

Even though he knew they were coming, William was surprised by the relatively quiet clank of the flash suppressed shots that came from JP's rifle. His excitement caused his left foot to slip out from under him and he slid down against the tree. He quickly repositioned himself just before the squall began.

Blood shot out of the back of the man's neck. His eyebrows rose for a moment and then, limp, he fell over.

One of the five remaining men in the house opened the door and stepped outside to look for his colleague. William and the three other US soldiers immediately fired at him. Most of the bullets hit their mark and the man fell to the ground.

Because the door was now open the remaining men

inside witnessed what happened and rose in a swarm of confusion and reaction. The tall one who had run out of the home earlier started firing indiscriminately through the doorway.

A few bullets whizzed by William and one hit the tree he was hiding behind. He thought that if they hadn't needed the prisoner they could fire on the small structure, or even toss in a grenade and kill all of those who were inside.

Miftah grabbed the thick tunban he was wearing, pulled it up and over his head and threw it down onto the fire, instantly extinguishing the flames.

The light in the tent went out, the silhouettes gone. Without saying a word to each other the four American soldiers simultaneously adjusted their night vision goggles. William wished that he had heat vision installed on his goggles. Night vision requires some light in order to work and there was now none inside the house.

They had previously agreed that William would stay

outside the building and cover the other three as they went in and engaged their targets. That process began as JP ran point and the other two followed. It looked as though they were actually running towards the house next door as William began firing at the open doorway in order to cover them. As soon as they were abeam the house they turned and ran along its front side. Once they reached the front door JP grabbed a flash grenade from his belt, pulled the pin, tossed it inside and yelled into his commlink, "Cover!"

A 170 decibel bang, designed to temporarily disorient their quarry, went off along with a bright white flash. For a moment William's own vision was obfuscated because of it. When his vision began to return he saw what looked like a shadow running from the back of the house.

"Shit," he said nervously into the commlink, "I think we have one on the run." They hadn't been told there was a back door or window on this structure.

"Engaged!" JP yelled back from the inside of the house. In the moment that William spent searching the forest behind the building for his missing suspect, the other special ops had run inside. An instant later loud gunshots rang out from the home. They weren't American.

A shape in the distance, made green by William's night vision goggles, caught his eye. It was definitely a person and he looked short.

Abruptly rising he yelled into his commlink, "One on foot, in pursuit…" and started running down the hill.

"We're a little busy in here," one of the soldiers

responded, out of breath. Whoever they were engaging inside were putting up a fight.

Though there was a Spectre gunship orbiting high overhead that could have supported with suppression gunfire, William chose not to have them engage because the enemies were in such close quarters to the Americans.

As he sprinted past the house William heard yelling from inside. He went up into the forest on the other side.

He could see Miftah's specter-like glow popping in and out of the spaces between the trees far ahead of him. He ran as fast as he could while keeping his target in view and not tripping on the rocky, tree root covered ground.

William hollered at the glowing green apparition, "Stop or I'll shoot!" in Pashto. But his target continued on as the sounds of men yelling receded behind him. The enemy gunfire seemed to have ceased.

"Stop!"

It was too risky to shoot at the running man's legs. If he missed and hit the guy's head or chest, he might die. If he did hit one of his legs the chase would be over, but the man might not survive the hike back to the landing zone.

Within seconds of yelling, William heard the sound of a gunshot from his left. Then another. The shots didn't come from the battle behind him. He had to consider that someone was firing at him.

Suddenly the green ghost went down. Tripping would be easy to do out here in the dark forest, William thought, especially after being exposed to a flash grenade. His rifle in front of him and his breath hurried, he yelled again, "Don't move and I won't shoot!" in Pashto.

BOOM! BOOM!

Another two gunshots blasted out from his left. He instinctively turned and fired two rounds out into the infrared-goggle-induced green sea when his original target rose and began running again.

"Stop!" He yelled, this time, mistakenly, instinctively, in English. The pursuit resumed, but this time the gait of the green orb of a man was more uneven. He must have twisted an ankle or a knee, William thought.

The distance between the two was closing. William estimated that he was only twenty yards from overtaking the runner as he subconsciously noticed the yelling from the engagement behind him had stopped.

The green orb disappeared. William scanned left to right rapidly while slowing his pace and raising his rifle. He could see nothing but green trees and his own arms in front of him.

Yet another two gunshots bellowed out from his left and this time he heard a bullet hiss by his ear. Again, he turned and fired without being able to see a target. He turned back to his original course just in time to see a large tree branch coming up from the ground toward his face. The speed of the branch was greater than his jogging pace. He hadn't run into the branch, someone was hitting him with it. Time seemed to slow as wood connected with goggle, helmet, bone and flesh. His neck snapped back as his gear went up in to the air behind him and his body headed towards the ground in an uncontrolled fall.

His mind was able to absorb an enormous amount of information in that instant. His back hit the rocky, uneven ground hard. Different rocky points hit several spots on his back like miniature Afghan mountains protesting the sky. Air rushed out of his lungs as his pupils shot open, trying to adjust to the lack of light. Without a target in sight, he lifted his rifle with his right hand and fired, but before he could get off a second shot the log that had met his face a moment before now met his hand... and his gun was smacked away.

Though he was having trouble catching his breath, he sat up and could now see his log-bearing attacker. He was short in stature, was wearing typical Afghan dress and had a scar along his right cheek. The log went behind the man's back sideways, like he was a baseball player preparing to hit a wild pitch, William thought. As he swung forward towards William's face, William simply lay back onto the ground and the log went soaring over him, missing its mark. The lack of connection caused Miftah to lose his balance and he stumbled. William noted this and knew it was time to strike, even though his own balance was still unsure.

He jumped up to a crouching position while yelling into his commlink, "Tailspin! Tailspin!" Tailspin was the previously agreed upon code word to call in the Quick Reaction Force. It would take those Marines a good ten minutes to reach William, but he knew they would find him fairly easily because of the Blue Force Tracker GPS device that was attached to his belt. Unfortunately his request would go unheard. The commlink system was also a victim of the log blow and was now smashed.

William reached out with both hands and grabbed Miftah's right leg. He then stood, bringing Miftah's leg with him. Miftah's left leg acted as a fulcrum as his right leg went up and his torso went down. William shoved the leg as hard as he could upwards and the man lost his balance and fell to the ground.

The sling that was wrapped around William's shoulder and was attached to his rifle had done its job. The automatic weapon dangled in front of him like a strange sadist's necklace. He grabbed the handle and the trigger with his throbbing right hand and lifted the barrel with his left. Instinctually he pointed the gun at Miftah's heart. Despite his head injury, William quickly remembered his mission, changed his mind and aimed for one of his legs. Pulling the trigger brought no reaction from the gun.

Surprised, he pulled it again. And again. The rifle wouldn't fire. Damage must have occurred when it was hit by the log

There was no time to try to fix the gun now so he reached down to his right pant leg pocket to pull out his knife. Before reaching the handle, he froze. Ten feet to his left was a tall Afghan man with a pistol pointed at his face. It looked to be an old pistol, William thought: a revolver with a long barrel.

Miftah noticed William looking away and then also

turned, looking to his right, to see what had grabbed his attention.

"Mohammad!" Miftah whispered, clearly relieved.

The man, Mohammad, began to squeeze the trigger. Time slowed again as William watched the cylinder of the .38 pistol begin to turn.

They had him.

"No, wait!" Miftah yelled at Mohammad.

2.

Smack, smack, smack! The plastic toy pirate sword William was using to attack a little bush outside of the front door of his house was on the verge of cracking. In his five-year old mind, he imagined this bush was some sort of monster who was trying to charge him. Leaves went flying with each strike.

His victorious feeling slipped away when he heard the sound of his father's car pulling into the driveway. Instantaneously he was transported from the world of destroying monsters to the world where little boys get punished for engaging in forbidden activities.

His father stepped out of the car dressed in slacks, a button down shirt and a tie. He looked as though he had come from some sort of business office, but he was, in fact, an Army doctor. Mostly he spent his working hours in a VA hospital attending to vets. But there were times in William's life where his father was gone for months attending to US soldiers in foreign countries.

William looked at the leaves on the ground and then at his father. Realizing what was probably coming next he froze with fear.

After stepping around the car his father saw the mess of leaves on the ground. William was standing next to the bush, looking at his feet, sword in hand.

"William Olson, why are there leaves all over the ground?" his father asked, surprisingly patiently, though the addition of their surname meant something was out of the ordinary.

After a pause, William responded, weakly, "The wind did it."

His father sighed and walked over to him.

"Bend over," he said to William calmly.

William complied.

His father lifted his hand in the air and brought it down, hard, on William's butt. An audible slap rang out and a nanosecond later a cry from William's mouth did, too.

"I told you never to lie to me!" his father yelled.

William started sobbing.

"Go inside," his father said.

He did and in the kitchen found his mother who, apparently, was oblivious to what had transpired just a moment before.

"What's wrong?" she asked, sweetly.

"Daddy spanked me," he responded between sobs.

"Aw, comeer." She lifted him into her arms and held him for a moment, then sat him on the kitchen counter. Smiling at him she asked, "Do you want a popsicle?" He nodded silently. She went to the freezer and retrieved a red and yellow Missle Pop. After removing the wrapper she handed it to him. He sucked on it while sucking snot back into his nose. Even though the popsicle was cold, he felt warm.

"It's when you put your lips together with a girl's lips and suck the air out of her lungs."

"No, it's when you lock your braces with a girl's braces and you are stuck."

"No way, it's when you put your lips on a girl's lips and then stick your tongue in her mouth."

All of these were answers to the question posed by William to his fellow fourth-grade boys, "What is French kissing?"

The debate grew hushed as a kid named Billy, a fifth-grader, walked over to the group to see what was going on. The playground at Madison Elementary School during recess was a segregated affair. The most desirable locations (the big slide, the monkey bars) were controlled by the sixth-graders, who were the oldest kids in the school. The next most desirable real estate (the bleachers, the drinking fountains near the janitor's closet) was owned by the fifth-graders.

The drinking fountain next to the boys' bathroom was where these inquisitive fourth-graders stood, pondering.

"What are you dorks talking about?" Billy demanded after arriving. All five of the previously high-spirited boys looked down at the ground and didn't say anything.

"What? What were you talking about?"

No response. Fear started to grip the boys. The difference in age between a ten-year-old and an eleven-year-old is like the difference between an eighteen-year-old and a forty-year-old. Billy's physical dominance frightened them. He had a reputation for stuffing younger kids into garbage cans just for looking at him.

Billy pushed William in the chest so hard he almost fell over.

"WHAT THE FUCK WERE YOU TALKING ABOUT?"

"We were trying to figure out what French kissing is," William blurted out before he had time to think. All of his friends looked at him, eyebrows slightly raised and eyes wide.

What had he done? Now Billy would think they were idiots. At best, he would tell the whole school what they had been talking about. At worst, all five of them were going home with broken noses.

William's friends stared at him. How could he have betrayed them? Their eyes went from William to Billy and back again. This was not going to be good.

Billy stared at William. William stared back. What could he do? Should he run? He would be teased mercilessly and called a pussy for running from a fight, but he knew he couldn't win a fistfight with Billy. His eyes went from Billy's eyes to Billy's right hand. He didn't know whether or not Billy was right handed, but it was likely. If Billy were to hit him, it would probably be with his right fist. "When Billy swings, I'll duck," he thought. "His fist will going flying over my head and he'll be off balance. Then I'll punch him as hard as I can in the nose. At least if I get my ass kicked, I'll have hurt him and no one can say I am a wimp."

William slowly moved his right hand behind his butt

and made a fist. Billy stared at him.

Inexplicably a smile broke out on Billy's face. "Ha ha ha ha!" he laughed.

"You guys are such idiots. French kissing is when you lock your lips with a girl and exchange bubble gum."

He turned and started to walk away, shaking his head. "Fucking retards!"

All of the boys seemed to exhale at the same moment. William could feel his heart beating in his head. After a moment Danny, his best friend at the time, said, "Do you think that's really true?"

"What's your fuckin' problem, loser?" Scott yelled at Graham. Though Scott was tall for his age, scrappy and confident, his enthusiasm and bravado were increased by the sense of safety he was enjoying. He was surrounded by a handful of other ten year olds who were all on his side.

Graham had no response. His beady eyes scanned the small crowd and then went back to Scott. Anger, fear, surprise and bewilderment were in those eyes.

"S is for stupid!"

The insult was in reference to Graham's blue, red and gold Superman shirt.

An odd fashion choice, William thought, for a ten year old boy who was pudgy, greasy haired and without ability in scholastics, athletics or making friends. Maybe he was being ironic?

William knew Graham must have been trying to formulate a plan for what to do next. As he watched a faint sense of nausea grew in his stomach.

The small alleyway behind Madison Elementary School was the ideal bottleneck for a trap. Both sides of the alley were covered in thick ivy, perfect for concealing ten-year-old boys hiding in wait. Wait they did, for what seemed like an eternity, William thought, for Graham to walk through on his way home from school.

William had no reason to hate Graham. None of the boys did, really. He was just one of those kids who was inexplicably picked on by all of the others.

Scott was mad at Graham for some trivial infraction (a pen borrowed without asking, for example, but it didn't really matter), and this infraction was the excuse for a beat down. William had never seen a fight in real life and was both excited and terrified about witnessing this one.

The semi-circle of boys surrounding Scott and Graham stared at them, waiting. Graham stared at Scott, waiting. Scott stared at Graham, waiting. William began to wonder if anything would happen. He felt as though the ivy surrounding the group waited, listening. The concrete below him wasn't moving despite his imagining it to be a moving stream. If it were a stream, the ivy on either side would be like the walls of a canyon. At the end of the alleyway would probably be a waterfall...

Scott broke the silence by suddenly lurching forward and punching Graham in the face. The sound of fist against cheek was disturbingly different from what William had expected. He'd seen men punched on television and in the movies many times. The punch was usually accompanied by a loud cracking sound. This definitely didn't sound like that. It was more of a fleshy, muted tap, but Graham didn't fall to the ground. His head simply turned to the right violently, accepting the punch and then snapped back. Graham looked back at Scott. Scott stared at Graham. The group stared at them both. The ivy stared at them all.

Graham put his hand to his cheek, which was now turning red. As tears started to well up in his eyes, he simply looked down at the ground and said

"Ow."

William felt a lump forming in his throat.

Graham slowly turned away from the group and started walking down the alley. Nobody followed. The boys stared at him walking away. The entire group felt defeated.

In an effort to break the trance, William blurted out, "Wow, that was cool!" He knew it wasn't. Deep inside he had hoped that he had missed something; that this really was cool and the other boys would explain to him why, but nobody responded. Everyone just stared, not knowing what to do.

William looked to the ivy seeking an answer that wasn't there.

"It wasn't a very clean hit," Scott muttered, analyzing his own boxing skills.

William watched as Graham reached the end of the alley, his hand still on his cheek and turned left, out of sight.

One, two, three. One, two, three. One, two, three, four, five.

As William walked along the suburban sidewalk of his hometown, he would try to make sure that he stepped an odd number of times in each concrete square on the ground. He imagined that underneath the sidewalk was a society of people who lived in the dark. If he stepped on one of the sidewalk squares, a light bulb directly underneath the ground would turn on and the people below would have light. If he stepped on the same square again, the light would shut off. One more step and the light was back on. It was important for the people to have light, so each square must be stepped on an odd number of times.

Walking in this manner required a bit of concentration and occasionally he would forget where he was or what he was doing. On this day he nearly walked into another boy standing in his path: a boy probably five years his senior, standing with his arms folded, looking down at him.

"Hey," the boy said, with a small smile on his face, clearly entertained by the fact that William almost didn't see him.

"Oh, sorry!" he gasped, his heart now racing and his face hot with embarrassment. He tried to pass around the boy to his right but the boy countered his move and blocked his path.

"Wait a sec!" the boy said.

"Oh, crap," William thought.

"You see that girl over there?" The boy pointed across the street. There were three girls about William's age standing together looking over at them.

"Which one?" William asked.

"The one with the pink sweatshirt."

"Yeah."

"She likes you."

"Oh, crap," William thought again. Though he was obsessed with girls and dreamt about kissing one, facing one in real life paralyzed him and left him longing for escape.

"Oh," he muttered. The two boys stood there looking across the street at the group of girls who were now whispering to each other and giggling. William started to panic and looked down at the ground.

After a moment he said, "I have to go do my paper route," and walked around the older boy. He could feel all of them staring at him as he walked away.

William's hands were black. The ink from dozens of newspapers, now folded and sitting in a pile next to him in his family's garage, had found its way from page to skin. The Times Tribune newspaper route to which he was dedicated was his first real job.

The Years Twitch

After standing up from his crossed-legged sitting position he grabbed the two empty canvas shoulder bags that he would soon be carrying and starting stuffing in the folded newspapers. After a few minutes, both bags were full and sitting next to each other, connected by the shoulder straps that eventually would be pulling down on him as he tried to ride his bike. He stood and waited for a moment, staring at those heavy bags. After gathering his courage, he squatted between them, one on his left and one on his right, and put the straps on his shoulders. Concentrating, he muttered to himself, "One, two, three… lift!" and he pushed himself up to a standing position, bags hanging on either side of him, his face red, his body simultaneously swaying and trembling. He tried to control his breathing, or panting, as he waddled over to his bicycle. This was the toughest part for him: getting one of his legs up and over the middle bar without falling over.

Standing next to his bike, William put his left hand on the handlebar, his right on the seat and prepared to mount. Again he concentrated. He had fallen over half a dozen times trying this maneuver in the past and thinking of his butt hitting the garage floor again made him anxious.

Very slowly and carefully, like a gymnast beginning a routine on a balance beam, he lifted one leg and put his foot over the bike. When it was down on the other side he let out a sigh of relief. The most difficult part was over. Once he gained some speed on his bike he would be fine. He just needed to start throwing papers to lighten his load.

With his right foot on the highest pedal, he pushed down as hard as he could and the bike slowly wobbled forward. When it appeared to be falling over to the right, he would counter by turning the handlebars to the right and pushing again on the pedals. If the bike started to fall over to the left, he'd turn left and push into it.

Finally he was heading down the driveway in a straight line. He had been concentrating so much he hadn't noticed the government issued sedan that had pulled up in front of his house. It was parked and two Army officers were getting out and putting on their service caps. They looked at him and he looked back at them. Their being there was odd, he thought, but they didn't call out to him. He really didn't want to stop if he didn't have to, so he kept pedaling down the driveway and out into the street.

The distraction of the officers caused him to almost run into a bush on the side of the road. He swerved and missed it, but paid for his mistake by having the canvas bag on his right side bang into his leg. That wouldn't stop him, he thought and kept pedaling. He imagined that the bush had reached out and tried to grab him, but he was too fast and smart for it.

Though the first few newspapers were thrown successfully and were now lying dormant on warm asphalt driveways, he was having trouble concentrating. Why were those Army officers at his house? His mom was home and would presumably speak with them but should he turn around? If the newspapers were delivered late he could get in big trouble. A knot started to form in his gut.

The knot grew worse as he became conscious of the fact that he was approaching the Murphy's house. Every time he rode his bike past their house their border terrier, Sadie, who was always sitting in their front yard unleashed, would bark, run after him and try to bite his ankles.

He started pushing his pedals harder. If he kept his speed up, Sadie usually couldn't catch him. As he approached the house he could see her sitting on the porch looking up at a nearby telephone pole. She hadn't noticed him and for a moment he thought she might be distracted enough by whatever was on that pole (probably a squirrel) for him to sneak past, unscathed. But just as he was passing the house, Sadie's head tilted down and her eyes met his. She sat for just a moment, looking calm, then started frantically barking while leaping from her sitting position and dashing across the front yard of the house. William started pedaling furiously.

Sadie's speed increased as she sped out into the street. The impossible pace at which the pads of her little paws skittered across the pavement was unnerving. Panting, William pumped harder and harder. Despite his efforts the distance between he and the dog was closing. Her shrill barks made the situation seem that much more desperate.

Bounding forward, Sadie finally reached him and tried to bite his high rpm ankles. She got a couple of nips in before she inexplicably put all four paws down to the concrete and skidded to a stop. Her barking continued, but she had apparently reached some imaginary border of her territory and would go no further.

William looked back at the barking madness receding behind him, sat down on his bicycle seat and coasted, catching his breath. A small drop of sweat found its way from his scalp to his hairline and then fell quickly down his forehead until it was wiped away.

The rest of the paper route proved uneventful. The papers were thrown and his bags got lighter, but he had trouble concentrating. The knot in his stomach wouldn't go away.

He pulled around the corner to his house and the sedan was notably absent. His approach to the house gave indication of nothing, yet he felt compelled to pedal faster. After skidding into the driveway he laid his bike down and ran inside, empty newspaper bags still on his shoulders.

He could hear his mother in another room crying and moaning. "Mom?" he cautiously called. His presence caused her to sniff loudly and clear her throat. "In here sweetie," she responded.

After entering their living room he found his mother sitting in his dad's chair, face stained with tears and mascara.

"What's going on?" he asked as his hands began to tremble and his face grew hot.

She motioned him over to her and once he reached her, she pulled him down and sat him on her left leg.

"It's Daddy. He isn't going to be coming home."

"Why not?"

"There was a helicopter accident."

William's reaction was strangely cold. He was aware that his reaction was odd as he was having it. Later in life he would feel guilty about not shedding tears, but thought that maybe his dad was helping him be strong from beyond the grave. He hugged his mother.

Even at this young age, he was aware enough to consider that perhaps he was in shock.

The pool party at Becky's house was one to which William felt fortunate to be invited. All of the most popular kids from his junior high school were in attendance, along with a handful of "B list" hopefuls. He considered himself a part of that latter group.

He found himself moving surprisingly easily among the kids. Any ice that was between them was broken when he completed a backflip off of a small diving board into the pool. Both the girls and the boys seemed to be impressed by this.

After toweling off he was enjoying eating Doritos in the kitchen with a few other kids when Becky motioned him to come over to her. She was standing in the living room in her one-piece bathing suit, still a bit wet from the pool. He walked over to her while chewing a mouthful of chips.

She cupped one of her hands around his right ear, put her mouth so close to it that he could feel her breath and then whispered, "Sara likes you."

He stopped chewing as his stomach turned upside down and his head lightened. This was fantastic and terrifying news.

"Really?" was all he could manage to say.

"Yep," Becky said out loud. "She just told me."

She stared at him, smiling. Not knowing what else to do, he lowered his eyes. After an awkward moment he muttered, "ok," and walked back into the kitchen.

He kept eating Doritos while trying to keep up conversation with the others. His mind was racing. He had always wanted to make out with a girl and it looked like this could be his big chance. Other opportunities had presented themselves to him now and then, but his courage had always failed him.

He fought the urge to leave that party.

Across the backyard of the suburban home, he could see Sara sitting in a chaise lounge laughing with other girls. Her blue eyes triggered a queasy nervousness in him. She was a little bit short, which was perfect for him as he was, too. For a moment he stared at her, half in a trance, half trying to figure out how he could make something exciting happen.

Without warning Becky ran up to Sara, cupped her hand over one of her ears and whispered something to her. Immediately Sara smiled and looked up. William ducked, not wanting to be seen.

Later the sun began to set and the pool water was finally still after hours of youth inflicted turbulence. Bathing suits were exchanged for jeans and sweatshirts as the air temperature dropped. William's heart rate had been so high for so long he was starting to feel exhausted. Loud music was playing in the living room as the crowd moved from outdoors to in.

William steadied himself against a wall of the living room and surveyed the group. Through the bodies he spotted Sara on the other side of the room. She looked over and caught his glance, which caused nausea in him. He looked away and tried not to shake.

When he looked back she was gone. A quick search of the room found her standing in a corner talking to Dirk, one of the really popular boys. In an instant jealousy, panic and rage created a fog through which William could hardly see. Dirk put his hand on her shoulder as they spoke: an intimate gesture that made William want to

The Years Twitch

vomit. But Sara looked around Dirk and across the room at William… and smiled. The fog lifted. He managed to smile back and then, not knowing what else to do, turned away.

This small exchange felt like a huge victory. Intimacy with a girl was new and frightening, but he knew he had to conquer his fear. Her smile was not coincidental or platonic and they both knew it. If he could capitalize on this moment there would be no rejection.

"Oh!" a boy near him suddenly yelled out. William looked over to see the boy smiling, but doubled over in pain, his arms wrapped around his stomach. Another boy standing in front of him had punched him. He was laughing, too.

"That was a good one," the slightly injured boy coughed. The boy who had thrown the punch was laughing hysterically. "You should see your face, it's all red!"

"Alright, it's my turn." The boy who had originally been hit suddenly threw his right fist forward into the other boy's gut.

"Oh!" the boy exclaimed, then doubled over and fell backwards. Most of the kids were now watching this exchange and collectively let out an "Oh!" when he was hit. A third boy exclaimed, "Lemme do it!" The first boy obliged him and hit him in the gut.

Within a few minutes most of the boys were paired off, punching each other in the stomach and laughing while the girls watched, shaking their heads. William looked around the room and found Sara sitting alone on a giant beanbag on the other side of the room.

Now was the time.

He walked across the room and when he reached her he said, "Can I sit with you?"

She smiled, replied, "Sure," and slid over on the bag. He sat down close to her, their hips and one leg touching. He wondered if he should say anything, but no words were making themselves available to him. Without warning he found himself leaning over and putting his lips against hers.

The slimy feeling of his tongue against hers surprised him. More than this, he felt relief. He had done it, he had made out with a girl. The triumph of this accomplishment distracted him from the matter at hand and he had to refocus on her. The moment he tried to bring passion back into the equation he felt a small panic: how does this end? How should he stop? Should he thank her? Should he just get up and walk away?

"Just focus on her!" he thought to himself.

As their tongues sloshed against each other their teeth occasionally tapped. He feared that since they both had braces they might get stuck together. Was that something that really happened?

A car horn honked outside the house. Somebody's parents were there to pick them up. William and Sara separated and looked up to find about half of the kids at the party staring at them. The kids immediately pretended they weren't watching by looking down at their shoes, starting a conversation with someone nearby or simply turning away. William felt embarrassed but proud. He looked at Sara and said "See you later." "Ok," she responded. He got up and walked out the front door to see who was honking.

Mike, William's best high school friend, had just turned sixteen and acquired his driver's license. The two were sitting in his barely running, grey Ford Grenada looking at the city below through the dirty windshield. The top of Western Boulevard was a curvy, gravelly affair with occasional large houses popping out of the trees that covered the hillside. The boys had found a fairly secluded spot that had a fantastic view.

Mike pulled a small pipe out of his right pant pocket and set it down on the maroon, fake leather bench seat to his right. He grabbed the air vent on the dashboard and pulled on it until it popped out. Inside the small cavity was a small plastic bag containing marijuana. After pulling it out he replaced the plastic vent into its hole and opened the bag. William looked behind them. The road was empty.

Mike broke off a bit of the pot and stuffed it into the small hole of the pipe. "I think that, even if you aren't sure if you believe in Jesus or not, you should be a Christian," he said, continuing an earlier conversation. "I mean, why not? If eventually you die and Christianity isn't real, it doesn't matter. You'll just be dead in the ground anyway. But if it is real, you'll get saved and won't go to hell." He reached in his left pant pocket and pulled out a small lighter. William shook his head, sighed and said, "Pascal's Wager."

"What?" Mike responded while putting the pipe in his mouth and lighting the pot with his lighter. He stifled a cough as the smoke entered his lungs.

"What you're talking about is called Pascal's Wager. Pascal was a guy from the 1600's who basically said what you just said. But he was wrong."

Mike blew the smoke out of his lungs and made the inside of the car mildly foggy. William rolled down his window as Mike asked, "How could he be wrong? What's the harm in being Christian, just in case?"

The pipe went from Mike to William and William sucked on it. The smoke immediately made him cough. Once he regained control he answered, "What if Christianity is the wrong religion? Let's say that God is real and he wants everyone in the world to be a Muslim. You've just spent your whole life being a Christian but you are going to hell anyway. How is someone supposed to know which religion to choose? All the major religions make incompatible claims."

Mike put one hand on each side of his own face and pulled back towards his ears. His nose flattened, his mouth stretched to almost twice its normal length and his eyes became slits. "They all make incompatible claims!" he yelled at William in a mocking tone. William started laughing uncontrollably until tears rolled down his cheeks.

Mike giggled a bit while staring out the front windshield at the panorama. "I don't know, I think what Jesus said makes the most sense." He took the pipe back from William and was about to light it again when William whispered, "Wait!"

Mike looked at him and saw that he was looking in the passenger rear view mirror. He turned his head back to see what was behind the car. It was an older lady, probably in her eighties, slowly walking towards them, the gravel under her feet crunching and giving away her approach.

"Shit, roll down your window," William loudly whispered. Mike complied as the woman came closer. William knew that if his mom found out that he had been smoking pot he would be grounded for the entirety of his remaining two years of high school.

The woman reached the car. Both of the boys started to shake with nervousness. It wasn't until later that they both realized the absurdity of being afraid of an elderly lady.

"Hi," she said once she reached William's open window.

"Hi, how are you?" William nervously responded.

"Oh, I'm fine. Listen, make sure you boys don't throw any trash on the road here. We've been noticing that people come up here to look at the view and then leave a mess."

"Oh, no problem, we won't leave a mess," William said while sitting up a little straighter.

"Good, thanks honey." She turned and began walking back the way she had come.

The two boys were silent as she slowly walked away. She was only about twenty feet away from the car when Mike looked back and grunted, "Fucking WHORE!" William immediately snorted and laughed so hard he couldn't breathe from the hilarity of 16-year-old irreverent humor. He looked in the rearview mirror and the lady was still walking away.

"What? You can't be serious?" Mike asked, incredulously.

"I'm serious," William responded, plainly.

The two just stared at each other for a moment. William's announcement that he wanted to join the Marines had caught Mike off-guard. The clamoring noise of students eating, talking, studying and generally milling about in the cafeteria at Petersburg Junior College continued, unabated, despite the sudden shift in conversational tone between the two.

"Are you nuts? They'll send you straight to Afghanistan!" Mike finally whispered loudly, as though someone might hear and judge them unfairly.

"I think that's where I want to go."

"For fuck's sake, why?"

"Think about it, I'm really perfect. I've been studying Central and South Asia for two years and can speak Pashtu and Farsi pretty well. I'm in great shape…"

Mike's eyes were wide.

"So?" he replied as he shrugged his shoulders and shook his head.

"I really think I could make a difference. They need people with brains in the military, not just dumbass high school dropouts. Being able to take it to the Taliban or Al Qaeda would be so…" William thought for a moment, then, looking down and slightly nodding his head, said, "satisfying."

"I thought you were studying languages so you could be a translator," Mike said, somewhat incredulously.

William didn't respond. The two just sat at the table. William staring down and Mike staring at William. There was a tugging in William that he associated with the brown cafeteria table, as if this piece of plastic and wood was urging him on, compelling him. A mixture of confidence and nervousness was stirring within him and he tried to codify these feelings as bravado.

The 9/11 attacks had only taken place a couple of years before, and William found himself trying to justify his compulsion through an association with that event. But he hadn't lost anyone close to him that day. Just as he was about to explain to his friend another reason, Mike interjected:

"Is this about your dad?" It was really more of a statement than a question.

"God made us, and made us with free will so when we love him it's our choice," Roberto said.

"But what about hell and the punishment for not loving him?" William replied. "That doesn't sound like much of a choice to me."

Roberto was quiet. William liked him for this reason. They could talk about religion or politics without getting too upset, which was unusual for most people.

Jogging had become easy for he and the other recruits at Camp Pendleton. William thought that the body has an amazing ability to adjust. He, Roberto and about forty other members of his platoon were on a five-mile run, and here he was carrying on a conversation. On his first day at boot camp six weeks ago, he had vomited from all of the running.

After considering William's question, Roberto replied through jog-induced heavy breaths, "That's not a choice that God wants to make either."

"But he has made a choice. He has chosen to say to us, if you don't love me, you go to hell."

"God does not want anyone to go to hell. That's his desire, but the choice to receive forgiveness is ours. His choice was to send his son in our place, so that our sins could be forgiven. God didn't dig us the hole we're in, but he offered a way out."

One of the recruits jogging in front of them looked back, rolled his eyes, shook his head and smacked a recruit next to him in the shoulder with the back of his hand. "The philosophers are at it again," he laughed as he pointed backwards with his thumb. The other recruit looked back and asked, "Why are you guys so into to talking about this stuff?"

"My dad is a minister," Roberto replied.

"My dad was a doctor," William added.

The recruit shook is head and muttered, "Great."

William felt frustrated. "I don't think you answered my question. If God really wanted us to love him through our own volition, why does he have to threaten us into doing it?"

Roberto was quiet. William then added, "If there really is a God I don't think he would have had my dad killed in a helicopter accident in Kuwait."

"Recruits, halt!" The bellowing voice came from the hill above them. They all stopped and looked up. Their drill Sergeant was standing with his legs slightly spread, hands on his hips and his campaign hat pulled down tightly on his head. "You all have exactly two minutes from this moment to get to the beach. If you are not there in two minutes you will not eat dinner tonight. Move out!"

William looked at Roberto and whispered, "God help us." Roberto chuckled and they began running.

Running over the bush-covered hills wasn't too much of a struggle, and William reminded himself that if he stayed calm and focused, he'd make it. As he rose to the top of a hill he could see the beach in the distance. As he descended to the bottom he would lose sight of it. When he came to the top of the final hill he could clearly see down to the beach and quickly became anxious. His drill sergeant was there standing next to a jeep, holding up a stop watch. Lying prone next to the sergeant were four telephone poles.

William was one of the first down the hill, almost falling when the downhill slope caused him to run too fast. Once next to the drill instructor he put his hands on his knees and panted.

"Twenty seconds left" the instructor yelled as more

troops made it down the hill and gathered around him.

"Ten seconds!"

Three of the heaviest recruits were nearing the bottom of the hill, their faces red, their mouths open and their gait erratic.

"Seven, six, five, four," the sergeant stopped as the last recruit stumbled in.

The sergeant smiled and said, "Well, well. You ladies actually made it! I have to confess I didn't think you had it in you. Since I'm so impressed I'd like to reward you. I'm gonna give you a half hour of break time. No running, no pushups, no marching. But I'm gonna need you to keep those telephone poles over there off the ground while you take your break."

Panting, the recruits turned and looked at the telephone poles on the ground a few yards away. Some of the young men looked down and shook their heads.

"What are you waiting for? Break up into groups of ten and get those poles off the ground!" the officer screamed. "The clock doesn't start ticking until all the poles are up!"

The recruits shuffled through the sand and surrounded the poles. William tried to calm his hurried breath. Knees touched sand, hands touched wood and anxiety grew in guts. All the young men were facing the same direction with William at the back. He decided to take initiative.

"Recruits ready!" he yelled.

"One, two, three... lift!" Grunts and snorts belched from the young men as the pole unsteadily went into the air and then onto their shoulders. Three other men in the same rear position as William got their poles into the air with similar strategy and struggle.

"If a pole touches the ground the clock restarts, ladies," the drill instructor growled.

The weight on William's right shoulder was immense. It flowed down through his spine, his hip, his legs and finally pushed his feet deep into the sand. Again he tried to slow his breathing.

Staring at a particular divot in the sand, he attempted to get into a meditative state. He paid close attention to his breathing and imagined the log flowing into his shoulder and giving him the strength of a tree trunk. Every time he would start to lose himself in a slight trance, the pole would wobble from one of his fellows losing strength and balance. This would snap him back to focusing on righting the wood.

Again he stared at one pocket in the sand. Eventually the sound around him diminished and his breathing slowed. He imagined that his tremulous shoulder was some sort of massage machine that was contending with, and comforting, his sore body.

The trembling increased so he began chanting a mantra to himself: "Suits are prison uniforms. Suits are prison uniforms. Suits are prison uniforms." He had decided earlier in his life that he couldn't stand working in an office wearing a business suit. Despite the pain he was feeling he was glad to not be in a cubicle under fluorescent lights. He was free… or relatively so.

The shoreline of Baja California was a confused mixture of stunning natural beauty and man-made grotesqueness. William and his three friends, Mike, Chris and Dan, walked along the water's edge, surfboards tucked into their armpits. Seemingly randomly, there was a rusted out Volkswagen Beetle half buried in the sand. Beyond it, closer to the fifty-foot cliffs that overlooked the sand and water, was a decomposing cow.

"God damn Mexico is a shithole," Mike said as they walked, looking up at the two heaps.

"Great waves though," Dan responded.

"Yeah, I'm exhausted," William added. They had been in the water for over two hours, surfing alone, save for a group of curious porpoises that passed nearby.

"Are there any waves in Afghanistan?" Dan asked William. They all looked at Dan, their mouths open and their eyebrows slightly furrowed.

"Dude, are you fucking retarded?" Mike asked, incredulously.

"What?" Dan responded, sheepishly. "It's not near an ocean?"

"Oh my god, you are retarded," Mike said as he shook his head.

"No, it's land locked," William said, smiling slightly.

This trip to Mexico was a last hurrah for the four friends. William would be flying out shortly after the trip. They had rented a relatively inexpensive house right on the edge of the beach.

As the four friends made their way up the bluff and onto the concrete road that ran along the edge, they passed what appeared to be a local standing on the other side of the street. With his hands in his dirty blue sweatshirt pockets he stared at them.

"Hola," William ventured. The man didn't respond. The rest of William's friends took notice of him. He was probably their age, dirty red baseball hat, baggy jeans, and dark, greasy hair falling out from the bottom of the hat.

"Wow, really friendly," Mike commented sarcastically.

The four continued walking up the street, until they reached the small driveway that led to their rental house. Dan pulled out a key that was wedged into the sleeve of his wetsuit and opened the front door. They walked inside. William was the last in and as he closed the door he looked across the street and saw the Mexican still watching him.

"That dude is still out there," he remarked.

"Throw some change at him," Mike said as he started pulling off his wetsuit.

"Dude, you are such a dick!" Chris exclaimed.

"What?"

"Everyone who lives in Mexico isn't poor!"

"Oh, right! You're telling me that dude standing out there isn't poor? He drags his sweatshirt and baseball hat through the dirt each day just to get that cool, poor guy look?" Mike responded as he peeled his wetsuit down to his knees. Chris noticed this, walked over and pushed him. His wetsuit being around his knees made him unable to stabilize himself and he started to fall. But before he did he grabbed Chris's arm and pulled him down. The two bodies created a slapping sound as they hit the floor.

Dan looked at them, and, shaking his head, said, "Get a room."

After the crew took their showers they reassembled on the balcony of the two-story house that overlooked the beach. Beers were popped open and Dan rolled a joint. He lit it with a cheap lighter, took a big lungful of smoke and then passed it to Chris. He took a big hit, fought back the urge to cough and then tried to pass it to William.

"No thanks," William said, raising his hand. Chris furrowed his brow and exhaled.

"Why not?" he asked, apparently slightly offended.

"I don't like it, it makes me feel paranoid."

"Just because you feel paranoid doesn't mean they're not after you. Go ahead."

"Wait, what?" Dan said.

There was a slight pause and then William agreed: "Yeah, that doesn't really make any sense."

"Dude, you are already high," Mike said to Chris.

"No I'm not!" Chris retorted.

"Yes, you are, pussy," Mike said.

The Years Twitch

"I'm not! I'm saying that they are after you, so you might as well smoke. Being paranoid won't change anything!" Chris exclaimed.

"Ok, you are high and retarded. Gimme that thing," Mike said as he reached his hand out to Chris. Chris rolled his eyes, shook his head and handed Mike the joint. "You guys are the retards," he muttered under his breath.

Stories of high school adventures were exchanged, facts were disputed and beers were finished. William got up and went into the kitchen to get more bottles for the group and as he did he looked out the window above the sink. The kitchen faced the street and from that vantage point he could see the Mexican, still standing on the other side, staring at the house. William shook his head and returned to the balcony.

"That guy is still out there," he reported.

"The dirty Mexican guy?" Dan asked. William nodded as Chris shook his head, offended by the description.

"Dude, get a life, we aren't going to give you any money," Mike said as he popped the cap off of his beer.

The late afternoon conversation bounced around wildly from subject to subject. Debate on gay marriage led to debate on video games which led to debate on what restaurants had the best French fries. Another joint was lit and offered to William, who regarded it derisively. He stood to go to the bathroom and on his way decided to look through the window in the kitchen again. The Mexican who had been standing across the street was gone. William leaned over the sink to get a larger perspective. When he looked to his right up the street he saw what looked like a cop car slowly rolling towards the house.

His pulse quickened.

Another few seconds went by and then he was sure. It was a cop car... Federales. Two of them in the car. And when they were across from his window they slowed, stopped and looked up at the house.

"Shit!" William said as he ducked. Hunching over he ran back to the balcony.

"Guys! Guys!" he whispered loudly. The three friends looked at him curiously.

"Throw the pot in the toilet! Throw it in the toilet! Now!"

"What the fuck dude," Dan protested. "Why?"

"There are fucking Federales out front! We've gotta hide!"

All of the formerly relaxed young men's eyes popped open and they jumped out of their seats.

"Fuck!" Mike whispered. Dan took the joint and went running, bent over so as not to be seen through any window, into the bathroom. William stayed low and a moment later heard the toilet flush.

Chris disappeared around a corner and Mike quietly opened the door to one of the bedrooms, went in and closed the door behind him. William heard two car doors open and close and then the voices of the Federales outside getting louder as they approached the front door. Crouched in the doorway of the balcony, he waited. He could see the front door from there. Would they bust it open?

The Spanish-speaking voices got close and William surmised they were in front of the door. The conversation stopped and a moment later the doorbell rang. William froze.

Silence.

Then a quiet, high pitched voice came from one of the bedrooms, "Nobody here but us chickens!"

A couple of snorts rang out from different parts of the house as the young men stifled laughter.

William was not amused. "Shut the fuck up!" he whispered loudly.

Bam! Bam! Bam!

The Federales knocked loudly on the door. "Policía!" One of them said sternly. William's heart raced. He absolutely could not get in trouble right now. He'd heard horror stories about Mexican police and their treatment of Americans, but what really worried him was that if he were arrested his military career would probably be over.

Then an idea came to him. The low table on the balcony was littered with empty beer and water bottles, empty potato chip bags and suntan lotion bottles. He pulled his T shirt over his head, threw it on the floor, then grabbed a half consumed bottle of water and poured it over his head. After taking a towel that had been left hanging over the back of one of the chairs he ran, head down, to the edge of the balcony and looked over. Two stories down the ground was covered with ice plant. He looked left, then right, and then saw what he needed: a thick rain gutter that ran down the back of the house.

"That better work," he thought to himself. He ran to the far right side of the balcony, threw the towel over his shoulder and climbed over the edge. He reached out with his left hand and put it around the gutter as his right hand still held the edge of the balcony. Trusting his instincts, he let go with his right hand and quickly brought it over to join his left on the gutter.

His hands burned as he slid down the gutter gracelessly and once he was only a few feet from the ground, jumped down. After landing unevenly he fell over onto the ice plant, relatively unscathed.

Next, he jogged to the side of the house, peeked around the corner and, seeing no one, caught his breath for a moment and walked casually around. As he made his way along the side of the house he tried to calm his breathing, but his heart rate wouldn't have it.

After reaching the next corner he walked around to the front of the house and saw the black and white cop car and, still at the front door, the two Federales.

"Hola," he said loudly to them. They both turned around, surprised. William knew a little Spanish. "Qué pasa?" he asked while smiling.

The two police officers turned from the door and walked towards him. They spoke in Spanish to him but the words went by too fast for him to really understand.

He attempted a response: "Me Español esta muy mal!"

One of the Federales tried some English, "You live here?"

"No," William responded, "just visiting! Vacation!"

The two Federales looked at each other.

"I was swimming!" he said as innocently as he could muster.

"You smoke pot," the other Federale said while staring hard at William, unblinking.

"Me? No, no pot for me!"

The officer just stared at William. After a beat, he pointed to the front door. "You open. We go look inside."

"Ah, I wish I could! I don't have the key!" William shrugged and held out his arms. The towel dangled from his right hand.

The Federales looked at each other.

"My friends must have gone to the store. I don't know how to get back inside!" He felt that his story was pretty weak, but the longer they were delayed out here the more the smell of the pot smoke would dissipate.

"You don't open door, you go to jail," one of the Federales said humorlessly.

William again shrugged his shoulders. "Senor, no tengo no llaves!"

One of the Federales sighed and lowered his eyebrows while looking at William as if to say, "Come on, this is weak."

"Pot in there," the other Federale said, pointing to the house.

"No, no!" William responded. "Cervezas, si! Pot, no!"

Again the Federales looked at each other. William's blood pressure escalated.

The three stood for a moment, not saying anything. This stalemate wouldn't last forever, William thought. They could get aggressive with him and, despite his military training, was outnumbered and wearing only swimming trunks.

"What's happening, guys?" Mike's voice came from behind William. William spun around to see him approaching in swim trunks, towel around his neck and a wet head.

"Ah, Mike, I was just explaining to these officers that I don't have key because I was swimming. You must not have a key since you were swimming, too, right?"

"Right! I just got out of the water," Mike responded as he reached the group, smiling. William noticed that his hands were red and there were bright red scratches on the back of his left leg. He hoped the police would overlook these details.

They did, but appeared annoyed. "¡Se abre la casa ahora!" one of them yelled.

"But sir, I told you, I don't have the key! No tengo llaves!" William shrugged and looked at Mike.

"I don't have any llaves either!" Mike offered, also shrugging his shoulders.

William attempted some more Spanish: "Nuestros amigos no esta aqui." He was trying to say that their other friends weren't there, but he wasn't sure if he had succeeded.

One of the Federales stroked the handcuffs that were attached to his belt. William noted this and looked at Mike.

"How was your swim?"

"Great. Yours?"

"Great."

They both looked back at the Federales.

The Federales looked at them.

The ivy in the front yard of the house looked at them all.
William began to feel that he was exerting a great amount of effort to keep from shaking. But that effort would inevitably cause more shaking so he breathed in deeply, as inconspicuously as he could, and calmed himself.
The Federales continued to stare and William and Mike just stared back, smiling slightly.

One of the Federales muttered something to the other, but William couldn't make out what he said. Again, the

Federale thumbed his handcuffs.

Without warning Mike let out a long, flappy, whoopy cushion-style fart. All four of the men's eyebrows shot up. William and the two policemen turned and stared at Mike in disbelief.

Mike's eyes were wide. "Sorry," he muttered.

There was silence for a moment as Mike was the target of their stares.

Then a snort came from one of the officer's noses. William looked at him and the man frowned, trying to hide a smile. The other officer put his hand over his mouth, obviously smiling. The first officer then lost control and started laughing hysterically, bending over in the process, hands on his knees.

The laughter was infectious and within a few seconds all four of them were cracking up. High pitched, girly squeals were coming from one of the officers, which made the other three laugh even harder, and, in turn, made him laugh harder.

"I…can't…breathe," William managed to say. The original officer who laughed had tears running down his face and wiped them away with both hands.

After a minute or two they started to settle down. One of the officers looked at the other and simply said, "Americanos." The other responded with his hands in front of him, palms up, "Americanos!" There was silence for a split second, and then the snorting and laughter started up again.

William put his hands on his knees, trying to catch his

breath. He knew they weren't out of this yet, but maybe the Federales would now soften their approach.

After everyone had caught their breath for a moment, the two officers just stared down at the ground, shaking their heads and smiling. One muttered something to the other in Spanish too fast for William to understand. Both shook their heads again, turned and started walking back towards their car. William and Mike watched them.

One of the officers waved. "Adios amigos," he said, with a smile on his face. The other, still smiling, went around to the driver's side and got in. William and Mike both waved back, dumbfounded.

The car slowly did a U turn, drove to a bend in the road and, once around it, disappeared from their view.

William turned and looked at Mike. "I can't believe you saved us with a fart."

Mike stared at him for a moment before responding, "Dude, I'm so fucking high right now. What the hell just happened? Seriously, I'm tripping the fuck out!"

The CH47 Chinook helicopter wasn't known for its luxurious appointments. There were no seats like were found on a commercial flight. He was seated on what looked like a long canvas gurney that ran the length of the inside of the helicopter. William was ashamed that only five minutes into the flight he was uncomfortable. If he couldn't handle this, how was he going to be able to handle the harsh Afghan wilderness he was about to greet?

Two special ops guys sat across from him on a parallel

gurney and one was next to him on his right. He wondered if they resented his being a part of this mission. Their previous two translators had been killed. Thinking of this gave William a nervous tingle all over his skin. He tried to convince himself that there was no jinx on this particular mission. The other guys just had bad luck.

Venturing a look out one of the nearby round windows revealed nothing to him but darkness. When they could, these helicopters flew at night, lights off. They were already incredibly loud and there was no reason to make themselves even more of a target to the Taliban or whoever was waiting below with an RPG or heat-seeking missile.

The helicopter shuddered slightly and a momentary queasiness in William's stomach signaled to him that they were descending. This was it. He took a big breath in order to stay calm. The big rotor blades seemed to get louder and once again he looked out the window. In the pale light of the moon he could see the grass covered ground below rapidly approaching.

The back ramp of the helicopter being lowered startled him and he regarded it with apprehension. As soon as it was fully open, he grabbed his backpack and started to rise. But JP, the special ops leader sitting next to him, grabbed his arm and pulled him back down into his seat. William looked at him with furrowed brow, confused.

"We're not getting off yet," JP said, shaking his head. William nodded in acknowledgement but didn't really understand what was happening. He looked out the window again and saw that the helicopter was hovering about twenty feet above the ground. Looking back at the other soldiers revealed nothing. They were simply staring straight ahead, waiting.

Though his heart was racing, William waited, too. After about a minute the ramp started to close and the helicopter leaned forward, taking off. Again he regarded the other soldiers, hoping for an explanation, but wasn't about to ask what was happening for fear of appearing to be a novice.

He was pushed back into his seat, then forward. The helicopter was making sharp turns, probably navigating through valleys. His fellow soldiers gave away nothing. These guys would be great at poker, he thought.

After a few minutes he felt descension, and, again, the back ramp opened and lowered. He looked at JP, who simply shook his head without looking back at him. William leaned back in his seat, now feeling slightly frustrated. The helicopter hovered for a minute, then the back ramp closed and they took off.

After a few minutes of flight, William could keep his curiosity at bay no longer.

"I'm sorry sir," he said suddenly to JP, "I don't understand why we are starting and stopping."

"Fake landings," JP responded, staring ahead. "If the enemy is watching we want to confuse them. We don't want them to know where we actually got dropped off."

"Ah," William sighed in acknowledgement. He felt stupid for not having figured out something that now seemed so obvious.

For the third time, the helicopter descended, hovered and opened the back ramp. William looked at JP expectantly and JP simply shook his head. Not yet. The ramp came back up and they took off.

William wondered how long this would go on. He didn't want to feel anxious, but not knowing when he was going to be let loose onto the battlefield was distressing.

Though it was dark in the cabin he looked up at the ceiling and noted the many wires and pipes running fore to aft, exposed, and wondered what they all did. What if he snipped one with his knife? Would the helicopter crash? Or would a heater, a light bulb or something else that was trivial stop working? He felt as if all of that gear had some sort of soul and was watching him but was emotionally uninterested in his fate.

Descent. He felt it in his gut, again. Looking out the window revealed the poorly lit ground approaching, again. And again the back ramp began lowering. He looked at JP, who was looking forward toward the cockpit. William turned and looked up toward the cockpit as well and saw the co-pilot simply lower his arm and give a thumbs up. William looked back at JP just in time to see him nod. He smacked William on the knee and said, "This is it, let's go."

All four of the men stood and jogged to the back of the helicopter. The loose ends of thick ropes that were attached to the ceiling were thrown over the edge of the ramp. JP held one of them with his right hand and with his left pointed at William. "Go," he said simply. William walked out to the edge of the ramp, grabbed the rope with both hands and stepped off the ledge quickly, before he could give himself time to think. He didn't want his nerves to get the best of him, as he hadn't descended a rope since basic training.

The noise and wind from the rotor blades was distracting as he slid downward. The ground met him faster than he expected and after stepping away from the rope, he went down to one knee, pointed his gun at the nearby tree line and watched for any movement.

A moment later what seemed like a hurricane of wind and noise nearly knocked him over as the helicopter lifted away. He looked over his shoulder to see the other men in similar positions as he was. As the sound of the Chinook echoed away in the distance JP motioned the men over to the tree line.

Quietly JP had the men note their position on their individual GPS devices so they could return, hopefully with a prisoner, for extraction. Then he showed them the position of the building where they thought they'd find the man they would later come to know as Miftah. It was due north of their current position. The men put away their GPS devices, snapped their night vision goggles onto their faces, and started slowly walking through the rough terrain.

3.

Click.

The gun didn't go off. Mohammad turned the gun in his hand and examined it, his eyebrows furrowed.

William simultaneously realized that his life had flashed before his eyes and finished pulling a knife out of his pant leg pocket. He leapt toward Mohammad using his injured right hand to clutch the knife as best he could. His left hand was in front of him, hoping to grab the gun.

Surprised by his advance, Mohammad's eyebrows went from down to up. He pointed the gun back at William and tried to pull the trigger, but he was too late. William was upon him and grabbed the gun with his left hand, twisting it, trying to get it released. With his right hand, he swung the knife toward Mohammad's torso, but Miftah intercepted the blow by seizing William's wrist. William had no control over the scream that left his throat from the pain of his probably broken wrist being grabbed by Miftah.

A violent dance began as Mohammad tried to free his gun from William's left hand grasp and Miftah tried to control William's knife wielding right hand. Miftah was holding William's wrist with both of his hands, trying to push the blade toward William's torso. But William was stronger and was holding him off, so Miftah let go with his right hand and tried to punch William in the face. William ducked and Miftah's hand went sailing over him. Miftah was then left trying to control William's right hand with his own left hand, which wasn't up to the task. William twisted his wrist free of Miftah's grasp and swung the blade toward Mohammad. Mohammad saw the blade coming and grabbed William's wrist, pushing the knife away from his torso. William held Mohammad's gun wielding hand up above their heads and Mohammad held William's knife wielding hand up above their heads. Mifta watched them both for a second, wondering if he should run for help or intervene.

William looked into his opponent's eyes as he tried to free his hands. Even in the dark night he could make out that they were small, dark and surrounded by leathery skin. A life lived in the harsh outdoors, plus a life of war, probably aged this man beyond his years, William thought. He was amazed at the details he could discern in a fraction of a second.

A blow to his head caused William's vision to blur and his balance to begin to fail. While trying to focus and hold himself up he lost strength in his hands and Mohammad freed himself of his grasp. William could hear the gun clicking and clicking, over and over, but it was clearly not going to fire. His eyesight returned just in time for him to see a small log rushing towards his face. He weakly tried to stop it with his hands but he was too late. The blow to the left part of his forehead wasn't as painful as the full body blow of the ground, which had rushed up behind him. His difficulty breathing was the last sensation he remembered when his consciousness abandoned him.

Small dots of varying shades of white enveloped his every sense. He could feel the dots making his entire body tingle and could see them dancing in front of his eyes. Intermittently he would drift from the dots to somewhere he'd been before, like a park, in the summer, playing tennis. His opponent on the court was his old friend Mike. But Mike wasn't speaking English, he was speaking Pashto, and he was uttering phrases like, "why don't we kill him?" and "we can make a video" and "it's too dangerous, others will come after him."

The dots were rolling him in a nauseating stupor. Gravity seemed to be unsure of whether or not it had any interest in him. In the brief periods of self-observation that were available to him, he knew he was hurt. His mind could not control his aching, limp body.

William looked around. White dots masked his peripheral vision while gravity lifted the ground toward his body and back away again in waves. Slowly the dots began to disappear and the room he was in started to right itself. Thought and pain rushed back into his awareness. He felt the inklings of panic as he realized he had no depth perception. But the reason for this soon presented itself: his left eye was closed. The momentary relief he felt after solving this small puzzle was extinguished when he tried to touch his eye with his left hand. It was bound. So was his right hand. More consciousness began to pour into his aching head. He quickly looked around. That's right, he thought. I was in a battle… hand to hand combat… two against one… maybe more than two?"

He was in a room with a dirt floor and mud walls and was sitting down in a chair. His hands were tied to the back legs of the chair. He tried to move his legs, but his ankles were tied to the chair's front legs. The aching in his head and right wrist increased when he tried to loosen himself from his bonds.

An urge to vomit became overwhelming. He slowed his breathing and tried to calm himself, but there was nothing he could do, it was coming. He turned his head over his right shoulder and puked on the dirt floor to his side. The sound of it must have alerted someone outside the room because William could now hear quick footsteps. The blanket that served as a crude door hanging over the entrance to the room suddenly flew open as Mohammad rushed in. He stared at William for a moment and then yelled in Pashto "He's awake!"

Another moment passed, William and Mohammad's stare unbroken, and then Miftah came in the room.

"Ah, great." he said, looking at William. "Samir will be back tonight with the video camera. This will be fantastic, God willing."

"I don't understand why you wanted to keep him alive," Mohammad asked.

"We'll kill him on video and post it for the world to see. We'll tell them that this is what happens to American soldiers who try to stop the Prophet's message."

William listened and assumed they didn't know he spoke Pashto. Miftah stared at William for a moment, then walked towards him. The hairs on the back of William's neck tingled slightly. Miftah stopped just in front of him, lowered his head until his face was only inches away from William's, nodded and said, in English, "American, you are thirsty?" William nodded. Miftah walked behind him. There was some sort of rustling going on, William could hear, and then Miftah returned with a small teacup. He put the cup to William's lips and poured in a little luke-warm tea. It didn't taste as though it had been tampered with so William gestured for more and Miftah complied. After he drank down the whole cup, William looked at Miftah. The two stared at each other for a moment before Miftah sighed and said, in English, "Stupid Americans, when will you learn?"

"Learn what?" William replied.

Miftah's eyebrows popped up slightly in surprise. He wasn't expecting an answer.

"This is not your country, you don't belong here," Miftah responded after a moment.

"You can say that again," William responded. Miftah smiled slightly.

"You come here, cause all sorts of problems… what do you expect is going to happen to you?" Miftah asked.

"You came to our country, knocked some buildings down, killed innocent people… what do you think is going to happen to *you*?"

Miftah leaned in again, "I think we'll keep knocking your buildings down, one by one, until there is no America left to poison the world."

"Poison the world?" William smiled. "I didn't realize that you are a comedian. Look how many people are trying to move to America. How many people are trying to move to Afghanistan?"

Miftah scrunched his eyebrows. "Co…median? What is comedian?"

"A clown," William responded. Miftah still didn't understand.

William tried again, using the Pashto word for clown. Miftah's eyebrows shot up in surprise, and then pointed down towards his nose as he understood the insult. He crossed his right arm in front of his chest, then swung it forward and slapped William's face with the back of his hand.

William laughed.

"You hit like a girl! Is that all you've got?"

Miftah leaned in again, "No American, there is much more coming for you." He stood up and walked angrily out of the room. Mohammad stared at William for a moment, then walked out.

The bonds on his ankles and wrists exacerbated the aching in his body. He sat, alone, for what seemed to be about twenty minutes without hearing a sound. The small amount of light spilling into the room implied that it was daytime. Fear began to well up from the pit of his stomach but he forced it back down by considering strategies. There had to be a way out of this, he thought, he just hadn't discovered it yet.

From outside he heard shuffling feet and then Miftah's voice. "Fatih!" he yelled. "Come here!" A moment later he heard more footsteps and then Miftah's voice again. "Stay inside with the prisoner." More footsteps and then the blanket door opened, momentarily letting sunshine pour in. Fatih, apparently, walked in. Thick, dark beard, headdress, tunban, machine gun... these guys all looked the same, William thought. Fatih sat down on the floor on the opposite side of the room from William and stared at him for a moment, then pulled the gun off his shoulder. William's anxiety at this action quickly ended when the man started pulling the gun apart, apparently trying to clean it.

After a moment William said, in English, "I need to piss." Fatih looked at him briefly, then back down to his gun.

"Fatih!" he yelled. This surprised Fatih and he stared at William with a quizzical look. William stared back and said in English, "I need to piss." Fatih lowered his eyebrows slightly, not understanding.

William had to consider his options carefully. If Fatih didn't know that he spoke Pashto he might be able to use that to his advantage. But this lone guard could be his ticket to escape. He went with his instinct and said, in Pashto, "I need to piss."

Fatih was clearly surprised. He considered William for a moment, and then said in Pashto, "You aren't going anywhere."

"Come on Fatih, what am I supposed to do?"

"Hold it."

"I can't. I've been here for hours. I'm about to piss in my pants."

"So piss in your pants."

"If I piss in here you won't be able to pray in here, the Q'aran is very specific about this." William didn't know if that was really true, but it was worth a try.

"Hold it."

"I really can't."

Fatih considered him for another moment and then returned to cleaning his gun.

The Years Twitch

William thought for a moment and then said, "Miftah is going to be really mad at you."

Fatih didn't look up from his gun.

Another moment passed and then William said, "Here we go," and starting pissing in his pants while staring at Fatih. Fatih muttered, "pig" and continued cleaning his gun.

Urine soaked his pants, butt and legs but hardly dripped on the floor. This strategy wasn't working, but he did feel relieved that he didn't need to piss anymore.

A sound like a firework going off far away caused Fatih to look up at William. A couple more pops and then what sounded like thunder made him jump up and run outside. William could hear several male voices, one of which was Miftah's, yelling near the room.

The sound of a distant battle was a relief to William. The thunderous noises were most likely M120 mortar rounds... American. He knew he had to get out of this room as he could end up getting bombed in there (not to mention decapitated on video if the Americans didn't find him). The battle was clearly a long way away, but if it moved closer there was no way for him to signal to his fellow Marines that he was in there.

The bonds on his wrists seemed to be leather and the one around his left wrist felt slightly looser than the other. He violently jerked against the tie but it wasn't coming undone. There was, however, about a half an inch of slack on that left tie. He tucked his thumb under his fingers, trying to tighten the circumference of his hand, thus making passage through the tie possible, but the bone that connected his wrist to his thumb protested.

Outside the sound of another pair of footsteps raced by and disappeared. The hairs on the back of his neck started to dance and William could feel death upon him. He knew he had to get out. Panic was rising in his gut. He had to get his hand through that strap, and the only way to get it through was to break some of his own bones. The thumb would probably break first, he thought. Some skin would be torn off and some of the small bones in his hand would be broken. But all of this would be a small price to pay for his life. It felt as though he already had a broken right wrist anyway.

Gathering his courage, he closed his eyes and prepared to break his own hand. It was the only way out. He took a deep breath then slowly started counting, "One... two... three!" With his left arm he pulled with all of his strength. His hand pushed against the strap for only an instant before it broke and his wrist went flying up in the air above his shoulder. His eyes widened as he looked at his relatively undamaged wrist. There was a bit of red rope burn where he would normally wear a watch but that was it. There were no extra broken bones. The strap was clearly weak and gave way under the pressure he had created.

There were more sounds of gunfire in the distance as he reached over with his free left hand and began trying to undo the double knot that was keeping his right hand bound to the chair leg. He always kept his fingernails short and now wished he hadn't.

This knot was stronger than the last. Frustrated, he pulled against the strap with his right arm, hoping to repeat the earlier success he had enjoyed with his other arm, but the leather wasn't budging and the pain from his broken wrist was too much to bear. Sweat dripped down his forehead and off of the end of his nose as he returned to the strategy of untying with the knot with his left hand.

"Come on!" he yelled at the knot, immediately regretting using his voice as someone outside might have heard. He picked and picked at it, but the knot was tight. Again, the sound of thunder rumbled in the distance.

His fingers red with wear and his face red from the struggle, the knot finally surrendered and loosened. He quickly pulled his arm free and bent over to start on his ankles. There was enough play in those straps that he realized he could probably slide the chair legs along his calves and free himself. And so his awkward dance with the chair began. In a half squat position, he pulled on the chair, trying to slide it upwards along his legs and through the ties. He lost his balance and fell backwards right back into the chair. "Fuck!" he whispered loudly, immediately standing back up and trying again. Eventually he got his left ankle free and then his right. The loose, unbroken straps remained tied around his ankles like bracelets as he stepped away from the chair.

This new freedom was exhilarating but he needed to make sure it wasn't short lived. With an aching head and pain screaming for his attention from what seemed like every part of his body, he ran to the blanket covering the entrance, pressed himself against the wall and listened. If someone came through that doorway he would have to dispatch him quickly and quietly. He heard nothing but more pops in the distance. After catching his breath for a moment he pulled back the blanket slightly and peered out. It appeared to be late afternoon. This room was one of a few small mud huts in a clearing in the middle of the forest. He could see no people.

The tree line was about thirty yards away and climbed

steeply up the mountainside. Before he ran from the room, he wanted to try to get his depth perception back. Pulling on his left eye gently, then firmly against the dried blood and swollenness, his eyelashes finally parted and he was able to see. The bruising around the orbit of his eye kept it halfway closed, but at least his eye was working. Taking a deep breath, he pulled back the blanket and dashed through the door. He ran in a zigzag pattern just in case someone started shooting at him. No shots came, though, and quickly he reached the trees and started his ascent. After jumping over rocks and logs and in-between trees for about forty yards he stopped and crouched down to rest for a moment. He dared to look back below and saw nothing but the handful of huts and no people.

Though he was free of his bonds, he started to feel the heavy weight of his predicament in his shoulders. Where was he? And where should he go? Should he run towards the sound of the gunfire? Showing up in the middle of a battlefield unarmed could be disastrous.

He remembered during his pre-mission briefings that the Taliban controlled home they attacked was essentially due north from his Marine base. This small village from which he'd just escaped couldn't have been too far from that building. He and his fellow Marines hadn't discovered this little village yet, so it was probably further north from the building. Therefore, he needed to begin a journey southwards to find his way home.

So which way was south? Afghanistan is a bit further south latitudinally than most of the US, but he concluded that during this time of year the sun would be somewhat to the south. It was difficult to find the sun through the thick trees but he was able to see enough shadows to get a rough idea. He couldn't find any moss on the sides of any of the trees, an indicator of which direction would be north, so he decided to make his best guess and start moving.

After taking only a couple of steps, he stopped suddenly, remembering that he had a small compass in his inside jacket pocket. He reached in hastily but the pocket was empty. In fact all of his pockets were empty, as was his belt. His Blue Force Tracker gps device that was attached to his waist before the battle was now gone. Clearly his former captors had rifled through his clothes and taken everything they could. He wondered if his fellow Marines were closing on his gps device now, wherever it was.

Snap.

William crouched behind a tree, hiding from the sound of a twig breaking in the distance. He peered around, looking for the source of the sound but saw nothing. He needed to get moving.

It was slow going through those trees and rocks. He had to keep his noise to a minimum, concentrate on not falling or twisting an ankle and keep an eye out for Taliban fighters all at the same time. He kept a steady pace, taking one or two steps, looking around, two more steps, looking around, etc. After what seemed like a small eternity he made it to the summit of a ridge. From there he couldn't see much down the other side as there were too many trees. The sounds of the nearby battle had abated, and he wondered who, if anyone, had been victorious. He began a descent down the hill.

The slope was steep enough that he had to be careful not to begin running out of control. Just as he began to fall into a routine of stepping and looking, he heard the muffled sound of men's voices in the distance.

Instantaneously he fell to his stomach. He was in a prone position, his head downhill and his feet uphill. It was uncomfortable but he didn't move a muscle. A small boulder was right in front of his face. The voices continued, but they were too muffled to be distinguishable. He listened intensely, hoping he would be able to decipher whether or not they were Americans. He stared at the rock that was an inch from his face and envied its stationary life. It stared back at him, he imagined, and wondered what on earth a human was doing there.

The voices were intermittent. Eventually they seemed to have stopped and William was about to rise and continue his journey when he heard a laugh. It was closer than he was expecting and his stomach tightened.

"You are a fool," he heard one of them say, in Pashto.

"You are the fool!" another voice responded, then laughed. William didn't move.

He could hear occasional footsteps, but no more voices.

His stomach began to get numb. Strange, he thought. He had experienced his foot falling asleep, his arm, his hand... but never his gut. His position was so awkward that blood flow to the skin over his belly was restricted. But he didn't dare move. While lying in that position he was able to look at his right wrist and hand close up. Both were very swollen... probably broken, he thought. With each heartbeat the pain in his hand pulsated. The excitement of his escape had temporarily blocked his awareness of the broken bones, but now the pain was making itself known to him loudly.

Slowly he leaned over onto his left elbow and peeked

above the rock in front of him. There wasn't anything but rocks and trees as far as he could see. He got up on his knees and looked all around. It was probably safe to start his journey again. The voices he heard sounded as though they had come from his left, meaning there was probably a path over there. The path wouldn't be a safe way to travel, but if he could keep it in sight he might be able to expedite his exit off this mountain.

Again he looked to where he was about to step, stepped, looked around, looked down again at the next step, and then repeated the whole process. It was an interminable way to travel, but he absolutely could not get caught.

After a few minutes the path came into view directly in front of him. He considered it for a few minutes, then turned about ninety degrees to his right and continued on, always keeping the path about thirty yards off of his left shoulder. This was dangerous. Someone could come bounding up the path and see him, but he didn't want to freeze to death, lost on that mountain. So he kept following it.

For the first time since his escape, he noticed how dry his mouth was. This was not a good sign. Dehydration was setting in. Just then he felt a grumble in his stomach. Hunger was entering the equation now, too. Going without food wouldn't be too much of a problem. Hunger would make him weak, but wouldn't kill him. But going without water would.

He wondered if his fellow soldiers were out looking for him. What happened in that battle that he left behind? What if he died out here from the elements? Would anybody ever find his body? He certainly hoped the Taliban wouldn't since they would use it for propaganda.

A crack of twigs to his right stopped him. His head snapped towards the sound. It wasn't too close, or he would have seen what caused it, but it couldn't have been more than fifty yards away.

It was too late to dive down and take cover. The noise from that sort of move would give away his position. William simply froze, staring in the direction of the sound. His heart was racing so hard he thought it might be audible in the forest.

Feeling like a statue, he continued to hold still. There was nothing moving anywhere around him that he could see. But he stayed motionless.

After a few more minutes he decided that an animal must have created the sound. If it were a Taliban fighter who created the noise William would likely be dodging bullets. There was always the option that the fighter was actually hiding from him, which struck him as slightly funny.

He took a tentative step forward and felt relief at putting his aching muscles into a different position. He looked back and forth between the area from where the sound originated to his right, the path to his left, and a few feet in front of him.

The perishable pace continued for hours as the temperature began to drop. William found himself unconsciously putting his hands on his neck, trying to keep warm. The light was getting dimmer and he would soon have to decide what to do when it got dark. Could he keep moving? He certainly didn't want to waste precious body energy going in circles. Sleep would be difficult, but helpful.

There was very little light left when he decided to try to get some sleep. He found a dirt area between two small boulders that was big enough to accommodate his body in a sideways, fetal position. Around him were plenty of pine needles and small branches. He slowly scooped them up, always looking back up and around, watching for Taliban. The little branches were scratchy as he pushed them into the collar of his shirt and around his neck, hoping they would help keep his heat from escaping. After making a small pile in the dirt for a pillow, he lay down and closed his eyes. He noted that the pain from his throbbing wrist had a bit of a rhythm to it.

Uneasy sleep had overtaken him, though for how long, he didn't know. He awakened in the dark, his heartbeat quickening while he listened for the sound of intruders, but he heard none. After shifting his body from one achy side to the other, sleep found him again, despite his new shivering.

Now and then a hard shiver would awaken him, but he heard no sounds around him that should cause alarm, so he would drift back into sleep. Occasionally he would dream that he had anxiously awakened and listened for the sound of danger, only to actually awaken and do the same.

When he next came to with a start, there was a dim light coaxing the forest around him to life. He thought he had heard a crack nearby, but he couldn't be sure. The trees bending slightly in the breeze throughout the night had created small noises that he had become accustomed to hearing and now failed to raise his alarm. But this crack sounded different.

Though well hidden, he could be discovered if someone were close enough. He heard a few more small cracks and the sound of dirt softly being displaced nearby. It felt as though his heart was actually in his head and was pumping so hard that his ears might shoot off, but he stayed still.

The sounds grew closer. Probably within a few feet, he reckoned. If he were found, he would have to act quickly. Surprise would be his ally as he would jump from his hiding place and hopefully disarm his opponent.

Air shot into his lungs as he gasped at the sight of a snow leopard leaping onto the small boulder directly in front of him. It was a small cat, probably two feet long and seventy pounds. William froze, hoping the leopard would not be startled and attack.

Transfixed by the cat's beauty and his desire not to tangle with it, William marveled at the brown and white fur with black and brown spots. Its eyes were a magnificent greenish brown surrounded by pure black that looked like eyeliner. Those eyes considered William's feet, and then moved to his legs, his torso and finally his face. The two regarded each other in an odd staring contest.

Fear drained from William's body momentarily has he watched the cat, mesmerized. Breaking the spell, the cat suddenly looked up and to its right as if it had seen or heard something. William became nervous.

The cat stared for a moment into the distance, then jumped down behind the rock. Its long spotted tail was the last of it William saw, and then it was gone.

He dared not get up, in case the snow leopard had been reacting to a man, or men, in the distance. So he waited.

Feeling as though he was hung-over, he finally could lay

no longer. He rose as slowly as he could, but his body was yelling out for a stretch. Looking around as he stood, there was no sign of the cat or anything else other than trees and brush. The path was still there, waiting.

After removing the somewhat ineffective branches and pine needles from his collar, he started off again; hoping scampering over rocks would bring his body temperature back up.

His head was aching. He knew this was because of his dehydration and that he had to find water soon if he was to survive. Though it was cold, there was no leftover snow lying on the ground from the previous winter. He listened for the sound of a stream but heard nothing but the distant rustling of the tops of the pine trees in the mild wind.

The slow journey continued despite his weakness. After reaching the bottom of small valley he ascended the other side, only to take another hour getting to the bottom of the next one. He was able to keep the pathway in sight, and ached to be able to walk on it and increase his pace tenfold. But it was too dangerous, so he climbed on.

There was a small clearing at the bottom of the next ridge, and when he reached it he risked exposure and walked a few feet out of the tree line into its small expanse. The sun was clearly in view here, though the fast-moving cumulous clouds moving across the sky occasionally obscured it. He turned his face towards the sun and let it warm him for a moment. Before long the need for alertness brought him back into the trees, and he watched.

His spirits were raised when he determined that, based on the position of the sun, he was, indeed, headed southward. The throbbing in his head and wrist pulled those spirits back down as quickly as they had risen. He knew he needed water. A couple of more days without it would be all his body could handle, if he was lucky. The high altitude was exacerbating his problems.

After staring at the path and the clearing for a few minutes, and, since he heard and saw nothing, and since the clearing was far too wide to go around with his energy depleting, he decided to race to the other side. Just as he was about to begin sprinting, in the distance he heard the sound of hooves on dirt. Instantly he pulled back into the trees and crouched down behind a hollowed-out stump.

After only a minute or so a small Afghan man and a donkey came around a bend in the path. The man's eyes were staring a few feet in front of him with one hand on the donkey's rein and the other holding a large cane or walking stick. They didn't seem to notice William.

The donkey was loaded with large packs and appeared to have been doing this sort of work for a long time. It's back was bent under and it's watery eyes were surrounded by grey fur. Its owner walked in a near trance, muttering to himself.

William waited.

The two passed by and out of sight, and long after the sound of the donkey's hooves were gone, William rose and decided, again, to make a dash across the clearing. He stood, took a deep breath, and sprinted out of the trees. His zigzagging pattern was unsteady but he reached the other side and jumped behind a small boulder, out of breath. There didn't seem to be anyone around who had noticed his movement.

Resting for a spell, he considered the forest. He was

hoping for some connection with the land and the trees, hoping for some inspiration that would aid his journey, but none came. Did the trees eye him with pity or cruelty? He couldn't be sure, and after a few minutes was ashamed of himself for wasting time trying to animate the insentient like he did when he was a child. He rose and started walking again.

Another hill lay in his path and by the time he reached its summit he was exhausted. After sitting uncomfortably for a few minutes on a rock, he noticed in the distance what looked like a clearing through the trees. He jumped up and advanced towards it. He knew that he was probably walking too fast, but he was excited at the possibility of getting a better perspective on his position.

As he got closer he realized that he was, in fact, correct. The trees came to an end at the top of a small cliff. Twenty or thirty feet below the path continued after winding down the hill to his left. At the bottom of this drop-off and next to the path was a small mud hut.

He sat and stared at the hut for a few minutes. He couldn't detect any movement inside and started to think that maybe it was the home of the man with the donkey. He waited.

After about twenty minutes he decided to investigate the hut. If there was water in there he desperately needed it.

The cliff face in front of him was too steep to descend, so in order to get down he would have to use the path. This was dangerous in and of itself but there didn't seem to be any other way. He began his small hike forty feet or so over to the path and then waited for a few minutes, crouched down. There were no sounds of donkey hooves or anything else in the distance so he stepped out onto the path and started walking briskly down towards the hut. After coming around a corner the hut was in view and he slowed his pace, trying to keep his footsteps quieter in case there was someone inside.

The hut looked similar to the one he had escaped. He slowly approached the now-familiar blanket door that hung over the entrance and listened. He heard nothing. He pulled back the blanket just slightly to peer inside, but it was too bright outside and too dark inside to see anything. He hesitated.

The thought of water was too much to hold him back so he briskly pulled back the blanket and rushed inside. It took a moment for his eyes to adjust to the dark interior, but once they did he saw a pretty typical Afghan home: a couple of toshaks and an old carpet were on the floor and a small dried mud shelf with some knick-knacks on it were against the wall in front of him. All of the walls were made of dried mud, but one of them was painted, surprisingly, bright yellow. William's head continued to turn from left to right as he took in the room. He found a small teapot on the floor and just beyond it a pair of dirty feet in sandals. These feet were attached to legs that were sitting cross-legged and were attached to the torso of a man. William lost his breath as he looked up and met the man's eyes with his own.

The man was old, wrinkled, dark brown and had a wiry beard that almost reached the middle of his chest. The beard was dyed an ugly orange/red color and he had a small multi-colored taqiyah cap on his head. William and the man stared at each other.

His body frozen but his heart pounding, William didn't move. If this man sounded some sort of alarm he was going to need to get out of there in a hurry. But the man continued, with his stone face, to quietly consider William. Instinctually William felt no threat, so he took a chance and, smiling slightly, nodded at the man. The man's eyebrows rose just slightly in response before he let out a long, peaceful sigh. He then reached over to a small wooden or cardboard box that was on the floor next to him. Again, William stopped breathing. If there were a weapon in there he would have to either pounce on him and take it or dive out the door.

The lid of the box was lifted, and the old man pulled out a small teacup. William's shoulders sank as relief flowed over him. He was still alert, however, watching the man and listening for anyone outside.

The old man picked up a teapot that was sitting next to the box, poured some tea into the cup and lifted it towards William. As he did so he nodded.

William slowly made his way over to the man and took the cup from him. The tea smelled odd to his western nose, but he took a tentative sip anyway. It was slightly bitter but having liquid in his dry mouth was practically intoxicating.

Not being able to resist, he gulped the rest of the tea down in one big shot. The old man smiled at this and reached out his hand for William to return the cup. He did and the old man refilled it and handed it back. Again, he chugged down the tea. Afterwards, he looked at the man, smiled and shrugged his shoulders. The man let out a small laugh and reached for the cup again. They repeated the whole scene two more times.

As the old man was refilling the cup for the fifth time, the two men both heard a sound in the distance.

Instinctively they both looked toward the door. It was the donkey hooves again. William glanced back at the old man briefly, then stepped toward the blanket door, pulled it back and ran through.

Deciding not to run straight back into the forest, he sprinted down the path away from the sound of the hooves. He needed to quickly put a lot of distance between himself and the hut. If the old man told the returning man about William, and if that man was sympathetic to (or a part of) the Taliban, he could be in a lot of trouble.

The circuitous path had him dashing around corners blindly. After a few minutes the risk of coming across someone hostile seemed too great so he once again crouched down in the forest two-dozen yards from the path.

A bit later he could sense no danger and heard no sounds, so he continued on his journey. Focusing on his steps he was able to get into a somewhat meditative state, using the throbbing pain in his forehead and wrist as a sort of metronome. The only problem was the fact that he was aware that he was trying to be meditative. At least all of this was helping to pass the time as he walked on.

As the sky started to grow from blue to amber, so too did anxiety begin to grow in William's gut. Though the tea the old man had served him helped, he was still very dehydrated and didn't look forward to another night shivering in the woods. Hunger was also affecting his every step and his concentration. He was weakening.

After coming to the top of a small rise in the forest he stopped and considered a new challenge. The path that he had kept in view now forked. One path led to the right and one to the left.

Squatting in the trees and gazing at the path, he hoped for some sort of sign or intuition to guide him. Nothing of the sort materialized and he mentally chastised himself for having indulged in such thinking.

After rolling forward for a few dozen feet, the pathway to the right climbed upwards and turned around a corner, out of sight.

The path to the left immediately began a descent and turned further to the left into the trees out of sight.

He once again risked discovery and ventured out onto the path, looked around and listened. There were no sounds of animals or people, but the whoosh of the wind in the tops of the trees sounded different than it had before, perhaps stronger. He tentatively approached the split point of the path looking both up the path to the right and down the path to the left. The whooshing sound appeared to be originating from below.

Trying to keep from being overly excited and keeping himself prepared for disappointment, he quickly walked to the edge of the left path. The terrain dropped off quickly below it and though it was hard to see through all of the trees there was a small river.

He could only see a small portion of it, but it was dark green with small stones poking through its surface causing little rapids. Though his sense of direction forced him to seriously consider the right path that headed up the mountain (it felt like it was the more southerly route), William stared down at the river, the path and the trees.

He thought hard for a few moments about which path to take and the potential rewards for having chosen the right one. But soon he could resist the pulling no longer and started down the path towards the river.

4.

Flying a Robinson R44 helicopter alone through the mountainous forest region outside of Denver was no easy task, even for a pilot as experienced as Ana Rollins. The steep, tree-covered mountain walls could extend as high as fourteen thousand feet from the valley floors below, an altitude impossible to reach in her piston-powered aircraft. The smart way to travel was actually through the mountains, but a lingering fog was making passage difficult.

Ana looked from the windshield down at her kneeboard chart. After matching a waypoint from the chart with what she was seeing outside on the ground she knew exactly where she was. However, the route she had chosen during her preflight planning, and marked on her chart with a pink highlighter, was now closed. The valley straight ahead of her was full of fog, and her little four-person helicopter didn't have instruments sophisticated enough navigate through it.

Another valley to her right seemed rather fog-less, so she looked down at her chart to see if it could provide an alternative route. After studying it for a moment, she decided that, though it would be a circuitous course and would add a lot of time to her trip, it would work.

She looked up from the chart to see a small puff of white cloud heading directly towards her.

"Shit!" she yelled out loud and immediately banked the helicopter to the right, avoiding the misty floating mound as if it were an asteroid.

Finding oneself in a cloud while flying a helicopter

without IFR (instrument flight rules) equipment is extremely dangerous. All sense of direction, both left and right and up and down, can be lost. Many helicopter pilots have inadvertently turned their ships upside down while inside a cloud, causing a sophisticated flying machine to become a brick.

Relief at missing the little cloud only lasted a moment as another larger cloud waited for her on her new course. This one was only a few dozen yards away and appeared to be too wide to go around. She instinctively lowered the collective (a stick to the pilot's left that resembles an emergency brake in a car and controls the rotor blades' pitch and rpm) and pointed the nose of the ship down in an attempt to go under it.

The forecast for today was supposed to be partly cloudy, but weather had a tendency to change quickly out here. She realized that fog and low clouds were actually forming around her. It was time for a go/no-go decision.

The rich real estate magnate she was supposed to pick up from his multi-million dollar ski home could wait. It was only a three-hour drive back to Denver for him anyway and he could afford a limo. Ana decided to go back the way she came and banked the helicopter to the right.

Only halfway through her 180-degree turn she saw another cloud heading for the windshield.

"For chrissakes," she muttered as she lowered the collective and the nose, continued her turn and ducked under the cloud.

Just as she was about to straighten out from the turn and start a new course back to her home airport she felt a strange sensation in her gut and a small vibration in her seat. Her eyebrows had just scrunched together, a result of her trying to figure out what had happened, when the low rpm horn went off.

Immediately and without thinking she lowered the collective further, twisted the throttle and pulled back on the cyclic stick. Her training had prepared her for a moment such as this and hadn't failed her. The horn turned off.

She tried to scan her instruments as calmly as she could: VSI indicated that she was descending at four hundred feet per minute. Rotor blade rpm was at 105% and slowly dropping. Engine rpm was at... zero!

Her engine had stalled. A gasp escaped her throat as she automatically lowered the collective even further, pulled back on the cyclic and adjusted her tail-rotor foot-pedals to get into an autorotation.

If a helicopter engine stalls, the aircraft doesn't just fall out of the sky. Pilots turn the rotor blades into a windmill and float down to the ground in a maneuver known as an autorotation, which is much like a plane without power coming down as a glider. But the pilot has to balance the descent rate with the forward speed, all while finding a place to land... within a few seconds.

Again, her training took over. She remembered that, in some cases, the best place to land might, in fact, be behind you. But in front of her, lined up just beyond the edge of her instrument panel, was what looked like a dirt fire-road.

"Perfect," she thought. During her training, she had practiced autorotations over and over. They had become second nature to her. That was the point: in an emergency situation being able to get down to the ground safely without overthinking was crucial. Ana was surprised at her own calm demeanor and the ease with which she was so far performing the maneuver. She even thought for a moment about why the engine had stalled. Without looking away from her landing spot she reached down with her left hand and felt the carburetor heat lever. It was not pulled out. Instinctively she looked at the manifold pressure gauge. It was below 17 inches.

"God dammit!"

Even during an emergency situation she was able to realize her mistake. Her carburetor had iced and stalled the engine. During her descending turn she should have added heat to the carburetor in order to keep the engine from being choked of fuel. She was so busy thinking about where to go and how to avoid clouds she'd simply forgotten.

Shaking her head slightly as she realized this ordeal was her own fault, she pulled the carburetor heat lever, intending to try to restart the engine. But her momentary distraction from flying the helicopter caused the low rpm horn to go off again.

"Dammit!" she yelled out while letting go of the heat lever and grabbing the collective stick. After righting the aircraft the horn stopped whining.

Her left hand abandoned the collective stick again as she grabbed the ignition key on the instrument panel and turned it. She could hear and feel a clunking, but the engine didn't seem to have restarted. A quick look at the engine rpm gauge confirmed this. It was still at zero.

She was within a few hundred feet of the ground now

and decided the best thing to do was to safely land. Once down she could figure out how to restart the engine and fly out, weather permitting. First she would broadcast a Mayday call. If there were any other aircraft nearby it was possible they could assist her.

"Mayday!" she said, surprisingly calmly, into the mic that was attached to her headset. "Helicopter seven zero two eight uniform has a stalled engine and is going down about four miles due east of Vail!"

There was no response. She had to refocus on her landing.

The part of curvy dirt road that she could see travelled from left to right in front of her. Surrounded on either side by tall pine trees, the road was not easily approachable on her current course. She was going to need to clear the treetops and then turn sharply to her left so that she was heading over the road like it was a runway. The problem with a sharp turn in a helicopter with no power is the loss of momentum in the rotor blades. She knew that if the turn was too sharp she could stall and fall out of the sky. If she didn't turn hard enough she would slam into the trees on the far side of the road.

As she descended and the tops of the trees grew closer, she was amazed at her thought process. She found herself angry for having made the mistake, angry for having sworn out loud by herself and angry for thinking of anything but making the autorotation successful. Additionally she was carefully considering her descent rate, wondering what was down in those trees and was conscious of her own thought process. She didn't think of these things linearly, one at a time. They all occurred to her at once, almost out of time.

She watched the tree line that was at the edge of the

road getting closer and closer, then looked back at her gauges. After making a few slight adjustments to the controls in order to keep her descent rate and her speed just right, her eyes were back outside and momentarily fixed on the road, then back at the gauges and then more control adjustments... just as she was trained.

Closer and closer the tree tops came and she had to force herself not to grip the controls too tightly. She had to stay loose and relaxed, she had to be steady. Beginner pilots would typically over-control an aircraft, paradoxically forcing it out of control. Ana told herself she was going to stay cool.

The edge of the tree line seemed to accelerate towards her until finally she reached it and passed over it by just a few feet.

"Goddamn, that was perfect," she thought to herself as the road appeared in plain view to her left and right and the tree line on the opposite side quickly approached.

This was it. She had to make a perfect turn. Her right hand pushed the cyclic stick to the left and the helicopter responded by banking to the left. The turn was steep and jarring.

Just as the road was lining up with the nose of the helicopter and she was about to pull out of the turn, the low rpm horn went off again. She had turned too hard. The rotor blades were stalling.

"No," she whispered.

5.

The toy department at J.C. Penney department store was a sea of brightly colored plastic. Ana's four-year-old mind was overwhelmed by the visual barrage and felt compelled to explore every piece. Like a bee confused by a window, she started to walk towards one toy, then stopped, turned slightly towards another and before reaching it, turned again, her attention captured by yet another.

Finally committing to one toy in particular, she walked directly toward it and grabbed it with both hands. It was a gold action-figure, a hulking, muscular man with a lion head, lying on brightly-colored cardboard that was covered with words and completely encased in clear plastic. It appeared that the arms and legs of the figure were movable, she noticed, but she couldn't get to them because of its clear plastic enclosure. Frustrated, she dropped the toy on the floor and looked for another.

A box of brightly colored rubber balls was within her reach on the bottom shelf. She picked up a pink one that was about the size of a tennis ball, squeezed it for a moment and then let it drop to the floor. It bounced higher and more effectively than she had expected so a smile broke out on her face. As the ball continued to bounce off the floor and into the air, lower and lower each time, she grabbed another ball from the bin and dropped it as well. The result was the same and the little girl's enthusiasm grew. She grabbed another ball and then another, dropping them on the floor and watching them all bounce. Laughter easily spilled from her mouth as she started grabbing every ball she could as fast as she could. The balls were rolling away from her in all directions when she pulled on the last one and dropped it on the floor while grinning. She didn't know which one to follow as they all set out on small journeys away from the box. It was as if they had been freed from a cardboard prison. The furthest escapee, the original ball she had bounced, was almost completely down the aisle and was about to roll around a corner. She watched it with fascination when suddenly she realized no one was stopping her. A rather adult sense of responsibility shivered up her spine. This wasn't something she should have done. She could be punished for this!

Quickly she turned around and looked down the aisle behind her. There were no adults in sight. She turned back the other way and found no people there either. The bouncing, rolling balls with their diminishing velocities were almost immediately of no interest to her anymore. What was of interest now was the location of her mother.

She hesitated for a moment, knowing that if her mother saw this mess Ana would most likely be in trouble. But fear and anxiety were growing in her belly as she started to feel very alone.

Tentatively she said, "Mama?"

There was nothing. Even the balls had come to rest.

"Mama?" she said again, this time louder. After a moment she walked to the end of her aisle and looked around the corner. She saw no people in that aisle either. Quickly the fear and anxiety in her gut grew so strong that she froze. It was as if her feet were stuck in cement that had just dried. Her physical weakness grew a sense of desperation deep in her body that pushed up into her head and took physical form in tears.

A small gurgle came out of her mouth as the crying

began. Tears streamed down her face, snot dripped from her nose and an uncontrolled "aaaaaaaa!" came from her throat. She simply stared down at the tile floor, unable to move but beginning to violently convulse with pure sobbing.

"Are you okay, little girl?" a deep male voice resonated from above her. She looked up to find an elderly man standing next to her, looking down and smiling. Still half frozen, she couldn't speak.

"Are you lost?"

She sniffed and stared, unable to do much else.

"Did you lose your mommy?"

She was finally able to softly nod her head.

The man reached out his hand, "Ok, come on, I'll help you."

She just stared at his hand, unable to move.

"It's ok, come on," the man said warmly, but she still couldn't react.

"Here, it's ok." He reached down and gently took her hand.

"This way." They started walking down the aisle.

His hand was warm but she wasn't immediately comforted. They approached a cashier as snot dribbled down from her nose into her mouth.

"Excuse me," the man said to the young, female

cashier. "This little girl appears to be lost. Maybe you could make an announcement?"

"Aw, sure," the woman replied to the man and then looked at Ana. "Don't worry sweetie, you'll be all right."

She picked up a phone, put it to her ear, pressed some buttons, and then, surprising Ana, spoke into the phone. But her voice came out from the PA system all over the store.

"Attention shoppers. We have a lost little girl at the cash register in housewares. If you are missing a little one, come see us!"

Ana stood staring at the white counter in front of her. She could feel the man and the lady looking at her.

"Aw, there you are!" her mother's voice came from behind her. Her inevitable arrival, expected by the adults, was a surprise to Ana, but her inability to move continued even when her mother picked her up.

"Where'd you go, silly?" she asked lightly. Ana just cried a bit more and put her arms around her mother, exhausted.

It seemed as if there were two ecological systems living side by side at the ranch on the shore of Lake Buchanan, Texas. The sandy beach at one end changed quickly into a grassy farm with oak trees within a few hundred feet. Ana and her single mother Tammy lived in a modest one-bedroom cabin near the water. The big ranch house up the hill was where Tammy worked as a domestic and farm hand.

Ana desperately wanted to pet the ducks that lived on the ranch. They waddled away from her in a casual manner every time she approached. A five-year old girl just wasn't a threat.

Like a domesticated dog chasing a quarry he'll never meet, Ana continually harassed the ducks. Their clipped wings kept them from flying away, but her daily attempts at handling them seemed to be regarded as little more than a minor annoyance. That was, until today.

The dozen or so ducks were being raised mostly for their meat. On this day Ana had been following them for about ten minutes straight when finally, after zigzagging up and down the beach, they ended up in the tree line. Three of the ducks unexpectedly turned, made an unusual honking noise and attacked.

Fortunately for her ducks don't have fangs. But they do have strong beaks and those beaks connected with her right arm, leg and the top of her head. The ducks made such an unusual ruckus that Tammy heard them from up the hill at the ranch home. Their quacks and honks were followed quickly by Ana's cries and screams.

Tammy ran down the path from the house to the beach as quickly as she ever had. She found Ana huddled in a fetal position on the ground, her hands covering her head, crying. The ducks surrounded her, quacking, many of them with their wings unfolded. A glance next to the bottom of a nearby tree brought Tammy the reason: eggs.

As she kicked at the ducks and scooped Ana into her arms, the loud honking and quacking was drown out by an even louder noise. Tammy looked up to see a helicopter zoom over them only a hundred feet above. She quickly headed back to their cabin, consoling Ana as they went. "You'll be okay, honey! You just got a couple of bruises. You scared the ducks because you got near their eggs! But good news, Jack is back!"

Once inside Tammy sat Ana on the edge of the kitchen counter and wiped away the tears from her big, blue eyes. "You want a popsicle?" she asked. Ana sniffled and nodded her head silently. Tammy smiled and went to the freezer. In the distance they could hear the buzzing of the helicopter winding down.

Jack Pierson was not only a ranch owner, but also a helicopter pilot. About a dozen years earlier he had discovered that it was much more economical to muster the cattle on his 20,000 acre ranch with a helicopter than with a huge crew of cowboys and horses.

Tammy handed Ana a missile pop and pushed her sandy blonde hair from her face. "See, you're ok! Don't let those nasty ducks scare you!" Ana didn't smile as she sucked on the popsicle.

Just as the buzzing sound of the helicopter got quieter and quieter and finally disappeared, a new rumbling made its way into the girls' home. "Oh, great," Tammy said to Ana, somewhat sarcastically. "Now we have to deal with those crazy cowboys!"

Once the cattle were pushed into a smaller area with the helicopter, the traditional cowboys on horseback took over to get them back into the pens. Ana could hear the hooves of the horses and the livestock, as well as occasional yelling from the dozen or so cowboys.

"You gonna be okay here for awhile by yourself? I need to go back up to the house to help Mrs. Pierson with dinner. There's gonna be a lot of mouths to feed tonight!" Ana silently nodded. "You just stay in here away from those nasty ducks, okay?" She nodded again. Tammy kissed her cheek and then walked out the door.

Ana turned and looked out the kitchen window to find the ducks wandering away from the area of eggs and the attack. They usually spent time down by the water, but she wondered why one of them wasn't sitting on the eggs. The chickens in the pens up the path seemed to always be sitting on their eggs.

She kept licking and sucking the popsicle absent-mindedly while staring out until she was sucking on the bare stick. She regarded it, chewed it a bit experimentally and then, having lost interest, set it on the counter.

After lowering herself down off the counter she made her way to the couch that hid a pullout bed on which she and her mother slept at night. She laid down on it in an upside-down fashion with her back on the bottom cushions, legs up the backrest and feet up over the top, staring up at the ceiling. This, for some reason, was her favorite position. In the faux wood ceiling above she would find shapes in the design and turn them into animals, usually fluffy, cute ones.

Her body exhausted from her avian ordeal, she soon fell asleep. She dreamt of being chased through a thick darkness by a giant carrot with fangs. Spotting a bedspread in the distance, she ran to it, dove under and held her breath. She could hear the footsteps of the giant carrot approaching. Finally the carrot reached her position and, apparently unable to see her any longer, walked right on top of her, unaware that his prey was so close.

She was startled awake by her mother's hand rubbing

her tummy. "Wake up honey, it's dinner time." Though she felt as though she had only been asleep for a few minutes, the darkness outside suggested otherwise.

The dining room in the ranch house was bigger than Ana and Tammy's entire cabin. Holding hands, the mother and daughter's entrance was hardly noticed by the hungry crew who had already begun devouring their food. The long table where they all sat reminded Ana of a picnic table, only it was made out of a fancier dark wood.

Jack was sitting at the end of the table. He was a physically imposing figure wearing a denim shirt with pearl snap buttons. On his head laid a mess of wavy grey hair that had recently been freed from the confines of his large brown cowboy hat. He looked up from his plate and saw them entering the room.

"Ah, Ana! Come over here and give Jack a hug!" Ana smiled at this recognition and affection and looked up at her mother. Tammy nodded, silently giving her permission and released her hand. She ran to him.

"There she is!" Jack said when she reached him. He picked her up and put her in his lap.

"How are you darlin'? I heard the ducks got tough with you today!"

"Uh-huh," she responded, looking down, shyly.

"Did they give you any bruises or cuts?

"Yeah."

"Where? Show me!"

Ana held out her arm and Jack noted the bruise on her forearm with exaggerated concentration and concern.

"That's a pretty good one," he said. "Any others?"

She pointed to her thigh. He noted the small purple bruise with the same amount of concern.

"That's another good one. Any more?"

She nodded and pointed to the top of her head.

He furrowed his brow and said, "Hmmmm… let me see."

He pulled back the hair on top of her head and examined it for a moment.

"Well, I count that one as number three. Any more?"

She shook her head.

"All right Ana, around here we have a one-quarter-per-bruise policy." Jack looked away from Ana and down the table at his crew.

"Isn't that right, boys?"

The men looked up from their food at Jack, expressionless.

"I said, isn't that right, boys?" he asked, more loudly this time.

One of the cowboys caught on. "Ah, yes, Jack! That's right! One quarter per bruise."

"Thanks Bobby," Jack responded. "At least one of you knuckle-heads has half a brain."

Jack reached into his pants pocket, rummaged around for a moment, pulled out some change and held it out to Ana.

"Ok sweetheart, take these." Ana complied and took the quarters from his hand.

"How many quarters you got there?" he asked.

Ana looked down at the quarters in her hand and counted.

"Three!" she responded with a big smile on her face.

"That's right!" Jack said. "Three quarters for three bruises! Does that make you feel a little better?"

She smiled and nodded.

"Good," Jack said. "Now give me a big hug, then go take a seat with your mommy at the end of the table there and eat some dinner, okay?"

She nodded, put her arms around Jack's big neck, squeezed, and then climbed down.

Ana walked behind the seated cowboys as they shoveled food into their faces as fast as possible. When she reached the last chair, which was empty, she climbed up. To her left was her mother, to her right, at the head of that end of the table, directly opposite of Jack, was his wife, Gracie. Gracie regarded her for a moment and made no expression. She simply sighed and then refocused on her plate.

As Tammy was loading Ana's plate up with food, one of the cowboys two seats down named Steven held up an empty salad bowl, looked at Tammy, and said, "Uh, Tammy?" Tammy looked at him and he shook the big salad bowl back and forth while raising his eyebrows. Tammy simply nodded, turned back to Ana, and said, "I'll be right back, ok? I have to go get more salad from the kitchen." Ana nodded in response and Tammy got up. Ana watched her walk away towards the kitchen.

When Tammy passed Steven, he turned and slapped her butt. She looked back at him, disgusted, and then looked up the table to Jack to see if he had witnessed the infraction. But Jack was in the middle of a conversation with his closest neighbor. She then looked to the other end of the table at Gracie, hoping for a different witness. It appeared that Gracie had seen what happened, but after noticing Tammy's glance, simply looked back down at her plate.

Ana wasn't sure what was happening, but she could sense the stress in her mother. Tammy looked back at the cowboy, shook her head, and said something that Ana couldn't discern, then continued on to the kitchen.

After dinner Tammy told Ana to go back to the cabin while she cleaned the dishes. She knew the routine. She was expected to be in her pajamas, teeth brushed and in bed by the time her mother returned.

On her way, Ana imagined the familiar, easy path to be moving below her, as she walked, like a treadmill… her position not changing. The world around her was moving, but she was staying in the same place. Like a person walking the wrong way down an escalator at the mall, if she stopped moving her legs, she would get caught on the world and ride along with it.

Once back home inside the cabin she hoisted herself up onto the kitchen counter near the sink and looked out the window. In the darkness she could just make out the area where the duck eggs lay but didn't see any ducks nearby. Again, she wondered why they weren't sitting on their eggs.

After brushing her teeth and putting on her pajamas, she pulled the three plaid seat cushions off of the couch and stacked them in their corner. "Stay!" she said to them, imagining that they were alive and if weren't instructed otherwise, would sneak away while she slept and eat all of her popsicles.

Next, using all of her strength, she pulled the squeaky bed, despite its protestations, from its clandestine enclosure within the couch. "Come on Donny!' she yelled as she yanked with her entire body. When the bed was finally out and horizontal she climbed up on it and said, "You aren't allowed to eat me tonight Donny." The couch was named Donny and Ana imagined that the bed was its tongue. When the alarm went off most mornings she imagined that she needed to get off of it because Donny was starting to get thirsty and needed to pull it back in.

As she pulled the thin sheets and old blankets that were already tucked into the small mattress over her, the bed squeaked. "Quiet, Donny!" she demanded.

Her head had just settled down on the pillow when she heard a duck quack. It sounded like it came from down near the lake. She resisted the urge to go and investigate, knowing her mother would be angry with her if she wasn't in bed upon her return. These ducks were becoming of increased interest.

A moment later, it seemed, the digital clock next to the bed was blaring an annoying morning radio show, pale sunshine was finding its way through the cabin windows and Tammy, lying next to Ana, groaned. She smacked the clock radio to quiet its rude interruption of her sleep and quickly resumed snoring. Ana looked to the corner where the seat cushions were stacked and felt relief at their still being there. She rolled back over and gently pushed on her mom's arm.

"Mommy."

No response.

"Mommy."

No response.

"Mommy!" she said again, this time a little louder and pushing harder.

After snorting, Tammy responded, "Uh, what, honey?"

"Donny's thirsty. We gotta get up!"

"Ok, honey, ok." She patted the mattress with one hand a couple of times and said, "Sorry Donny, we'll get up now."

Within an hour Ana found herself back in the dining room in the same chair as the night before. All of the same people from the night before were in their same chairs as well. The whole scene's only major change other than sunlight was the smell of eggs, bacon, newspapers and coffee instead of barbecued ribs, beer, dust and male body odor.

Again, Gracie Pierson regarded Ana with no emotion and quietly ate her food.

When the biscuits started to run low, Steven, the man who had troubled Tammy the night before, held up the nearly empty bowl that housed them and looked down the table.

"Tammy!" he said, smiling.

Tammy regarded him for a moment, then slowly wiped her lips with her napkin, set the napkin on the table, stood, walked along the backs of the sitting cowboys towards the kitchen and, when she passed him, stepped wide, out of his reach.

A few moments later she returned with a new bowl full of biscuits. She walked directly to her own chair, sat down and offered the bowl to Gracie. "Mrs. Pierson," she said respectfully, "would you care for another biscuit?"

Gracie simply shook her head without looking at her. Tammy turned the other way and passed the bowl to her closest neighbor.

After everyone seemed to be finished eating Jack spoke loudly over the din of light conversation around the table, "All right boys, let's get a move on." The cowboys all responded by standing up and stepping away from the table.

"Ok honey, go feed the chickens while I clean up," Tammy said to Ana. Ana simply nodded and climbed down off her chair.

"See ya later, Tammy!" Steven said with a big smile on

his face. Tammy shook her head and started picking up dishes, not responding.

Ana rode the path treadmill until she reached the chicken pen. As she expected, the chickens were sitting on their eggs, undistracted by her arrival. A silver pail half full with feed hung next to the pen on a nail and she took it down. She grabbed four fistfuls, as Jack had taught her, and threw them into the pen.

As she stepped down from the pen she could hear Jack's helicopter coming to life in the distance. She walked the rest of the way down the path to the lake and the cabin to find the ducks on the beach next to the water.

She felt an uneasy truce with them, but they regarded her with suspicion. Or so she thought. After going into the cabin she walked into the kitchen, lifted herself up onto the counter, climbed over the sink and looked out the window. The ducks eggs were unattended. She stared at the eggs for a few minutes, feeling concerned. Then a small smile broke out on her face.

She climbed down off of the kitchen counter, walked to the front door and stepped outside. The ducks down at the water seemed to notice her but didn't react in a discernable way. Ana walked to her right, the direction away from the eggs and walked around the corner of the house. She looked back at the ducks, who didn't seem to be paying attention to her. After walking along the side of the cabin, she took one look back to make sure the ducks weren't watching her, and then slipped around the back.

After walking behind the cabin and reaching the other side, she peered around the corner but couldn't see the ducks, as the beach was not in view from this perspective. She crouched down and tip-toed away from her house towards the eggs.

She walked slowly and carefully, making sure to not create any sound that would give away her movement. A few minutes later she had reached the eggs.

They looked similar to the eggs she had seen her mother working with in the kitchen, only a little greener and slightly speckled. There were nine of them but Ana quickly and softly picked up only two. With one egg in each hand she turned quickly, staying crouched down and tip toed, much faster this time, back toward the cabin.

Once she reached the back of her home she sprinted to the other side, then, nearly skidding out and falling over, turned left, ran up the side of the house and, instead of turning left again to go to the front door, turned right and began dashing up the path toward the big house. After a couple of steps she looked back at the ducks. They were still at the water's edge, apparently unaware of her pilferage.

She ran up the path as fast as she could without risking falling. Out of breath when she reached the chicken coop, she stopped and looked inside to find the hens walking around the floor eating the feed she had thrown in earlier. Carefully she held one of the eggs between the thumb and first finger of her right hand while using the rest of her fingers to open the squeaky wire and wood door of the pen.

Once inside she quickly walked over to one of the nests and looked down to find a pile of chicken eggs. She looked back at the chickens, who seemed not to notice her and then turned back to the nest and placed the duck eggs gently down in it.

The Years Twitch

She stepped back and admired her work like a painter looking at his canvas. Her satisfaction was soon interrupted by the sound of Big Jack's helicopter rapidly approaching. This always excited her so she dashed out of the pen and onto the path just as he flew over. She squealed and sprinted down the path toward the lake as fast as she could, hoping Jack would give her a show today. As she navigated the turns of the path, the noise from the helicopter was not abating. She knew he was waiting.

As she sprinted around the last corner the lake came into view and there was Jack in his helicopter, hovering just a few feet above the water. She screamed and waved her arms frantically, hoping he would see her. He did, and waved in response. Then he spun the helicopter around twice, all the while making a cloud of water spray out towards the shore from the rotor blade downwash. She laughed and jumped up and down. He straightened the helicopter out, waved one more time, then turned and flew away. She watched him and the craft float higher and smaller into the blue sky until they were gone.

After catching her breath, she decided that her work was not finished. She walked back up to the cabin, then along its side and around the back. When she peeked around the corner the coast appeared to be clear. She ran to the duck eggs and crouched down. After picking up two she used the same route back to the chicken pen.

Within a half hour, all nine of the duck eggs were mixed in with the chicken eggs in the nests of the coop.

That night the routine of Jack and the cowboys returning, dinner in the dining room and Steven being an asshole repeated. Ana couldn't understand why Gracie never smiled or said much. She stared at her face, trying to solve the mystery, not realizing, as small children never do, that staring is impolite.

Without warning, Ana blurted out, "Are you sad?"

Gracie's eyebrows shot up in her biggest show of emotion that Ana or Tammy had witnessed to date. She stared at Ana while the rest of the table grew quiet.

"Ana!" Tammy scolded in a loud whisper. Before Ana could respond, Gracie smiled slightly and said, simply, "I'm fine, sweetie." Then went back to eating her food. The rest of the diners looked for a moment and then turned their attention back to their food and their conversations.

After dinner Ana walked down the path towards the cabin and stopped at the chicken pen. She smiled at the site of the hens sitting on the eggs, apparently asleep. Satisfaction was growing within her as she pulled herself away from the pen and headed home.

Once inside the cabin she looked through the kitchen window at the area where the duck eggs had been. Though it was dark, she was pretty sure that the adult ducks weren't there. Her sense of satisfaction grew stronger.

Her nightly routine resumed as she brushed her teeth, put on her pajamas and pulled out Donny's tongue. In the distance she could hear some yelling, laughing and glass breaking. It was the cowboys, she surmised. Every now and then they would get loud after drinking too much "koo koo juice," as her mom would call it.

The couch squeaked upon Ana's entrance and was summarily scolded. The cushions, piled in the corner as usual, were warned to stay put and shapes of animals were searched for in the ceiling.

Before too long Tammy returned home and upon closing the front door and, finding Ana awake said, while shaking her head, "Those crazy cowboys are drinking koo koo juice again."

"Why do they do that?" Ana asked.

"It makes them feel like children, which I think they like," Tammy responded and walked into the bathroom, closing the door behind her. Ana could hear the sound of water running and teeth being brushed.

A few moments later Tammy came out of the bathroom and got into bed with Ana, who scolded Donny for squeaking. She then put her head on her mom's chest.

"Time for you to tell me a story, mommy," Ana demanded.

"Oh, sweetie, I'm so tired right now. Why don't you tell me a story?"

"But I don't know any."

"Sure you do. Or just make one up."

Ana thought for a moment.

"Ok, once there was a duck named Love, and he was the cutest duck who ever lived. He had purple feathers and was very, very good at baking cookies."

"Ooh, that sounds like a nice duck."

"Yes, and he could also bake cupcakes."

"Uh huh."

"And also, doughnuts."

"How nice."

"And also, spaghetti."

"Wow, that is quite a duck."

"Yeah, and also candy."

"He could bake candy?"

"Yes. And, popsicles."

"This sounds like an amazing duck, did he…"

Tammy's sentence was interrupted by the sound of a bottle breaking on the ground outside followed by a man's laughter. Both Tammy and Ana's bodies jumped as if they had been shocked by an electrified cattle prod.

Ana leaned up and looked at her mother, who said, "It's ok sweetie, it's just the dumb cowboys." But the fear in Tammy's face betrayed her words.

They could hear gravel and dirt crunching outside. It was footsteps getting closer.

"Hey Tammy!" a male voice yelled out from nearby. This startled Tammy so badly that she jumped out of bed, picking up Ana with one arm. It sounded like Steven.

"Come on, sweetie," she said in a loud whisper and carried Ana over to the living room closet. After opening the door, she set her down underneath the bottoms of the coats and dresses that were hanging inside.

"Ok baby, you hide in here until I come get you. Ok? Don't come out unless I get you. Don't make a sound."

"But mommy, why?" Ana protested as the urge to cry welled up in her startled throat.

"Just do as I say, baby," Tammy said as she began to close the closet door. Before it was shut, there was a loud knock at the front door. Ana saw her mother jump at this as the closet door closed and darkness surrounded her.

"Tammy! Open up! I need to talk to you!" the male voice yelled from outside. Ana could just barely hear her mother's feet shuffle away over the sound of her own galloping heartbeat in her ears.

A drawer in the kitchen opened and closed.

"Tammy!" he yelled again, then banged on the door. There was no response.

"Come on, I just want to talk to you." For a long moment there was silence.

"I know you're in there, I can see the light! Open up!" There was a moment of silence and then a series of very aggressive bangs on the door. Ana hugged her knees to her chest as her body began to tremble.

He aggressively rattled the locked doorknob and then yelled, "Open the fucking door you dumb bitch!"

Ana heard the telephone in the kitchen being picked up off the receiver. A moment later she could hear her mother whisper, "Jack, I'm so sorry but..." Ana couldn't make out the rest of what she was saying.

Bam!

Steven must have slammed his body against the door, trying to knock it down. This caused Tammy to involuntarily scream and begin to cry.

Then there were a couple of more big hits against the door.

"Let me in, you fucking whore!" he screamed and bashed into the door again. Ana was trembling.

Tammy said nothing, but Ana could hear her moving through the room.

In a calmer, sweeter-sounding voice, Steven said, "I'm sorry Tammy, I'm just a little drunk. Come on out here and talk to me. I just want to talk to you. I want to get to know you better."

Tammy said nothing. Ana could feel the bottoms of coats and dresses on the top of her head and hoped they would drop and cover her up if anything bad happened.

"Tammy?" Steven called out.

Boom!

Another body hit to the door caused Ana's trembling to double.

"Open the fucking door! If you don't open it I'll kick it in, you fucking idiot!"

Just as Steven had finished that sentence there was a thunderous explosion somewhere outside. Tammy screamed, Ana jumped and outside the door, Steven exclaimed, "Jesus Christ!"

Ana could hear quick footsteps in the gravel and dirt outside heading toward the cabin.

"Get away from that door, Steven." It sounded like Jack's voice.

"Whoa, Jack," Steven responded. "Don't point that thing at me!"

"Get away from the door."

"Easy, Jack, I was just…"

"Move it!"

"Ok, ok. Just stop pointing that thing at me."

"I said move it!"

Ana could hear the sounds of footsteps retreating from the cabin and Steven's voice, trying to explain away what he had been doing.

And she could her mother quietly crying.

"Mommy?" she quietly ventured. The sound of sniffling and shuffling feet followed and then Tammy opened the closet door.

"Sorry about all that, sweetie," she said as she lifted her up and held her. Ana wrapped her legs around Tammy's midsection and her arms around her neck. Despite her best effort Tammy started to sob. Ana did, too, for a moment, then regained her composure and started stroking Tammy's hair.

"You'll be ok, mommy."

Tammy laughed and responded, "Thanks baby. I know. I just got a little scared, that's all.

The next day the breakfast routine played itself out again, only there was no Steven. His chair sat empty. The conversation was less robust than usual and Ana felt slightly uneasy.

After breakfast she walked down the path and stopped at the pen to feed the chickens. They were already wandering around, knowing it was time for food. She spotted the duck eggs in the nest and simultaneously felt satisfaction and relief. After tossing in the feed, she turned and found her mother and Jack coming down the path towards her. Jack clutched a pillow in his right hand.

Before Ana had time to consider her bemusement, Jack said to her, "Ana, do you want to go for a flight with me this morning?"

Shaking with excitement she looked to her mom for permission. Tammy simply smiled and nodded. Ana jumped up in the air and squealed. Jack laughed. "Is that a yes?"

She yelled, "Yes!"

"Ok then, let's go!"

She emphatically responded "Ok!" and ran along side him. He laughed and the two began walking up the path. Tammy watched them walk away and tried to bury the worry in her heart. She had to confess to herself that she felt a little hurt that Ana didn't say goodbye, but this was a forgivable offense. The sight of a large man wearing a cowboy hat, carrying a pillow and walking with a little girl was humorous enough to calm her.

As the two passed the main house, Ana noticed Gracie peering out one of the windows, glaring. Ana looked from the window up to Jack, but he didn't seem to notice his own wife.

She regarded the pillow in Jack's hand again, and then asked, "Where are we going?"

He smiled and looked down at her, "We're gonna fly down to the south end of the ranch. There are a few dozen head of cattle down there that we need to bring back home so we can do some tests on them to make sure they are healthy."

"Oh, ok."

They walked through some small oak trees and around a curve in the path to find an open field where Jack's helicopter sat, its rotor blades drooping, looking like a giant bug sitting, waiting, in the morning sun.

Excitement welled within her. When they reached the aircraft, Jack opened the passenger door, put the pillow he had been carrying down on the seat, then reached down, put both of his hands under her armpits and lifted her up.

She couldn't restrain a little giggle as he placed her down on the pillow.

"How does that feel? Can you see out the windows, you think?" Jack asked. She nodded enthusiastically, smiling.

He then pulled down the headset that would make communication between the two possible while the noisy engine was running. He put it on her head, made some adjustments, and then leaned back.

"Ok, how does that feel?"

"Good!" she responded, still smiling.

"Well, this is easy, you're a natural pilot! I've got to check a few things out before we start up and get out of here, so you just be a good girl and sit here and wait for me, ok?"

"Ok!"

He walked to the back of the helicopter and started examining the engine as a part of his preflight ritual. While he did, Ana looked closely at all of the dials and switches on the instrument panel. Her insatiable curiosity was making it hard for her to sit still. She desperately wanted to know what all of those things did. The helicopter had dual controls, so there was a control stick directly in front of her. Without thinking, she instinctively reached for it and just as she touched it, Jack opened the pilot side door, startling her.

"Don't take off without me, Ana!" he said, seeing her fingers on the control.

She jerked her arm back, wondering if she would be in trouble, but he just smiled.

"It's ok. That's the cyclic stick. Go ahead and grab it while the engine is still off."

She did.

"Now, if you want the helicopter to go forward, just push it forward, away from you."

She just stared at him.

"Go ahead," he said, still smiling. "Push it!"

She looked back at the stick, curled the fingers of her right hand around it and then pushed it forward.

"Good!" he exclaimed. "And if you want the helicopter to go backwards, just pull it towards your chest. Go ahead."

She pulled the stick back.

"Very good! If you want the helicopter to go to the left, just push it to the left. If you wanna go to the right, push it right."

She pushed the stick left and right a few times.

"See, it's not so hard!" he said. "You pretty much just point the stick wherever you want to go."

She nodded and moved the stick around some more, like she was stirring a pot of soup.

He laughed, took off his cowboy hat and lifted up the bottom cushion of his seat. There was a storage compartment underneath and he deposited the hat inside.

"I wish I could wear that while I fly," he sighed as he put the cushion back down and climbed into the cockpit.

"Ok, Ana, no more touching the controls unless I tell you it's ok. Right?"

"Ok," she said, releasing the stick.

He put on his headset, fastened his seat belt, flipped a few switches and then started the engine. It made a coughing sound similar to a car starting. Then the rotor blades started slowly turning. She watched them coming round and round again over the front of the cockpit. Soon they were spinning so fast she couldn't make out an individual blade. They blurred into what almost looked like a solid disc.

After flipping a few more switches and pulling a few more levers, he said, "Ok, you ready to go?" She simply looked at him and nodded. He nodded in response and then, very slowly, the ground fell away from the helicopter. The nose lowered and they started moving forward.

Ana felt obsessed. She desperately tried to take mental notes as fast as her small mind would allow, not wanting this possibly once in a lifetime experience to be lost to a future, older Ana. The stickiness of the leather seat on her bare leg, the movements of the dials and gyros on the instrument panel, the small movements of Jack's feet and hands and the resulting movement of the entire aircraft, the new perspective on the ranch from the air… all of these encounters where quickly and decisively being absorbed by her, but the physical consequence of it all was one of a nervous shake. Jack noted this and queried her, "Are you all right?"

She looked up him, smiled and quickly nodded, then turned her attention back to the windshield, afraid of missing something significant.

Jack turned the helicopter so that they were following the path from the house down to the cabin at an altitude of about one hundred feet. She was surprised at how small everything looked, including her mother, who stood near the cabin and waved as they flew over. Ana waved back and before she knew it, Tammy was behind them and the lake had shot underneath their feet. Dark blue was below them and light blue was above. Ana was pushed down into her seat as Jack pulled back on the stick and the helicopter's nose pitched up. The two rose into the air simply, effortlessly.

Ana was surprised at how smooth the ride was. She felt as though she were driving in her mother's car. The higher they went the less she noticed their velocity.

"You wanna take the stick for a minute?" Jack asked after leveling out at about 1,500 feet. Her eyes widened as she stared up at him. After a moment she simply nodded.

He laughed a little and said, "Ok, then, grab the stick. I'll be on here with you so don't worry." She put her hand on the control.

"Do you remember what I taught you before we left?"

"Yeah."

"Ok then, give us a left turn."

She pushed the stick to the left a little too hard and the helicopter banked aggressively.

"Whoa!" he exclaimed as he leveled out the ship.

"Sorry!" she said, smiling.

"That's ok darlin'. Let's try it again, but this time be a little more gentle."

"Ok." She pushed the stick left again, this time with such a small amount of force it didn't seem like the stick actually moved. The helicopter gently leaned to the left and started a shallow turn.

"Wow, you are a natural! Very good! Now straighten us back out."

She did.

"Ok, let's try a right turn."

She pushed the stick right and the helicopter followed, but the nose started to slowly point downwards.

"The nose is starting to sink," he said. "So pull back a bit on the stick and keep us level through the turn."

She pulled back a bit too hard and they started to climb.

"Easy now, not so hard."

They repeated these exercises a couple more times before he said, "Ok, now take us in a big circle to the left." She complied and made a shallow left turn that took them east, north, west and finally south again. Once they were back on their original course, she straightened the ship.

"Guess what Ana?"

"What?"

"You did that all by yourself!" Jack said as he held up his right hand, proving that he wasn't on the control. She smiled and laughed a little.

His paternal praise over even the most trivial of her accomplishments gave her a warm feeling. Even at her young age she was aware that his compliments were exaggerated, though not entirely disingenuous. For her the most valuable part of their exchange was his interest in her happiness, which was clearly genuine.

The two confidants continued on their southerly course of one eight zero in search of the herd.

The blade of grass disappeared into the ground. Even when Ana pulled at it and got as close an inspection as her human eyes would allow, she still couldn't envision what the ant, walking next to it, could see. She imagined that far above her some frustrated god was trying to see the freckles on her arm.

While lying prostrate, half in the dirt and half on the grass that lined the path from the cabin to the main house, she picked a few pieces of grass and, squinting, looked at them as closely as she could. Her inspection process was disrupted by a ruckus that seemed to emanate from the chicken coop.

Dropping the small blades of grass, she jumped up and sprinted towards the pen to investigate. Mixed in with the loud sounds of the hens squawking were quieter, high pitched and sadly pathetic-sounding squeaks. Fear vibrated down her neck and through her arms as she quickened her pace.

She threw the door to the pen open to find a horrendous scene. Two of the hens simply sat on their nests, squawking. But one was down on the floor, wings spread, driving her beak, again and again, into the twisted body of what appeared to be a dead duckling.

Ana gasped as she quickly surveyed the rest of the scene. The chicken's eggs were still in the nest, unhatched, as were the rest of the duck eggs; but one duck egg was cracked open at the top, and small duck head and part of its right wing were sticking out.

The hen obediently moved out of the way when Ana ran into the pen. She grabbed the duckling from the nest as gently as she could, cupped it in her two hands, turned around and ran back towards the door of the pen, stepping over the area where she thought the dead duckling lay, unwilling to look down.

Tears began streaming down her face as she scrambled back towards the cabin.

The Years Twitch

"It's ok, it's ok," she breathlessly said to the squirming duckling, trying to sound reassuring.

In the distance she could hear her mother yelling from the main house, "Ana?! What is going on? Ana? Where are you?"

A few moments later Ana awkwardly opened the door to the cabin with her elbow, trying not to squish the duck, who was beginning to make a squeaking noise and push itself further out of the egg.

Once inside she ran to the couch, set the egg and duckling down and stepped back, her eyes wide and her chest heaving up and down. The duckling continued to squeak and wriggle out of the shell. In the distance the sound of the angry hen subsided.

After the duckling freed itself from the confines of the shell, it flopped around on the couch wildly. Ana was frozen, not knowing what to do. Just as the thought occurred to her that she had better run and get her mother, the door to the cabin flew open and Tammy rushed in. "Ana! What's happening?"

"Mommy! Help it!" Ana screamed, pointing at the duckling. Tammy's eyebrows shot up into her forehead as she gasped. Before she could say anything, Ana ran past her and through the front door.

"Where are you going?" Tammy bemusedly demanded.

"I'll be right back!"

She sprinted back up the path and halfway to the coop started to lose energy. The anxiety in her gut, anxiety about the duck eggs, demanded that she keep moving. She in turn was demanding more energy from her little legs. They could deliver little more than increasingly painful cramps. Her gait turned into something resembling a drunken walk.

When she finally reached the coop she swung the door open and found the hen simply standing still on the floor near the dead duckling. The other duck eggs in the nest were unmolested and showed no signs of birth.

Panting, she carefully entered the coop, trying to keep from looking at the dead duckling by focusing on the duck eggs. She stepped over the area where she thought the mess to be and, after reaching the edge of the nest, stood for a moment to catch her breath.

Once her muscles began to calm, she lifted the bottom of her shirt out in front of her with her shaky left hand. With her right hand she picked up the first duck egg and placed it gingerly into the basket she had created with her shirt.

She turned and looked down at the murderous hen and found no reaction, so the next egg was loaded into her shirt. Another glance at the hen found no change in her disposition, so another duck egg went in.

A few moments later all seven of the duck eggs were in her improvised basket. Slowly she turned, staring down at the eggs with wide eyes. The hen was motionless.

It was not easy, but she split her concentration between gingerly handling the duck eggs, stepping over the dead duckling, not antagonizing the hen and moving with a pace that would insure the eggs' arrival at their proper nest before they hatched.

The path seemed to have grown in length as she carefully tried to hurry down it. As she approached the cabin, she could hear the duckling inside squeaking away. In a surprisingly mature act that betrayed her years, Ana passed the cabin and walked straight back to the nest area where the eggs had originally been found. Once there she slowly, lovingly, pulled the eggs out of her shirt one at a time and placed them in the twig nest that still sat against the bottom of the tree.

"Love."

"Love?"

"Yes, Love."

"The name of your duck is 'Love?'"

"Yes!" Ana responded to her mother, exasperated, as her eyes rolled back into her head.

"Ok, ok," Tammy conceded, laughing a little. "It's just an unusual name, that's all."

The two sat at the edge of their bathtub watching Love swim around while squeaking and putting its head quickly under water and pulling it back out again. In the week since she had been born, Love seemed to have doubled in weight.

The fate of Love's siblings was simply not discussed. A couple of days later, Ana tentatively entered the chicken coop to find the entire mess had been cleaned up. The benefactor responsible for this never revealed himself or herself to her. She felt a sort of bond with this benevolent person, whoever it was. Asking around to discover the identity of this person would be a betrayal of that bond.

The punishment she expected for the whole ordeal never happened.

Another week later her curiosity about the other eggs finally got the best of her so she walked to the tree where they had been left. Curiously, the eggs and the entire nest were gone. Again, for fear of both being in trouble and causing her benefactor to possibly reveal his or her identity, she never asked anyone if they knew what had happened.

.

"Will you buy us some beer?" Ana's matter-of-fact tone was disarming to the homeless man.

"Uh, what?" he responded.

"Beer," she said, a little too clearly and condescendingly. "We'll pay you if you buy us some."

Ana and her friend Sarah were standing around the corner of one of the only two liquor stores in the little Texas town of Buchanan. The sixteen-year-olds were on a Saturday night mission. Rumor had informed them that the town bum could be talked into buying beer for kids.

The man, who was sitting against the wall, his dirty belongings next to him, stroked his ragged beard and considered the offer.

"Hmmm... I don't know."

Ana impatiently pulled a twenty-dollar bill from the front pocket of her blue jean shorts and held it in front of him.

"Here's twenty dollars. Buy us a 12-pack and you can keep the change."

The man stared at the money for a moment, then slowly, apparently painfully, stood and gently took the money from her hand. Without a word he limped away from the girls and around the corner. Ana and Sarah looked at each other with wide eyes. Could it really have been this easy?

"What if he runs away with our money?" Sarah asked.

Ana pointed to his belongings. "All of his stuff is here. I don't think he'll bail."

The two girls looked around. Living in a small town had certain advantages, like a lack of traffic. But there were disadvantages as well. If they were observed by a friend of one of their parents who happened to drive by, the freedom they were currently enjoying would be at an end.

As the sun set, the cruel Texas humidity loosened its grip on the inhabitants of this modest borough. Above the girls the formerly blue sky was full of pink twisted clouds and to the west a fiery orange hue was losing its brilliance. The welcome relief of night was beginning to close in on them.

"James told me he is going to be there tonight," Sarah said as she quickly raised her eyebrows up and down. Ana responded by rolling her eyes.

"God, I'm not that into him!" she responded dramatically.

"I think he's pretty into you!" Sarah said with a smile on her face.

"Whatever," Ana said looking down, unable to hide a slight smile.

Sarah gasped and looked out at the road. Ana, startled by this, turned to see a sheriff's patrol car drive by. She looked back at Sarah.

"Do you think he saw us?"

"It doesn't matter, we aren't doing anything wrong."

"We just gave a homeless dude twenty bucks to buy us beer!"

"The sheriff doesn't know that!"

"He will if dufus homeless guy walks out and hands us a freakin' twelve pack!"

"If the sheriff comes back we're getting in our car and leaving. The homeless guy just got a free twelve pack. Or better yet we'll walk in the store and buy a pack of gum or something."

Ana got nervous.

"Where the hell is he anyway?"

Just as Ana finished that sentence the homeless man walked slowly around the corner carrying a brown grocery bag. Ana and Sarah's eyes darted from the man to the street, anxiously watching for the arrival of the sheriff.

It seemed like an eternity for the man to reach the two girls and when he finally did, Ana grabbed the bag from him while quickly saying thank you and ran to Sarah's car. Sarah opened up the hatchback of her small Honda and Ana dropped the bag in. As the girls got in, buckled their seatbelts and started to drive away, Sarah said, "I can't believe you thanked him!"

"Why shouldn't I thank him?"

"He's a crazy homeless guy!"

"So? He still helped us. And he's still human!"

"Helped us? We helped him! He just earned money from us!"

"We helped each other. God, you are such a snobby bitch!"

Sarah simply shrugged her shoulders and kept driving.

"I've got to get out of this heat box of a state," Ana said while rolling down the window of the air-conditionless car.

"Tell me about it," Sarah responded. "I think I'm going to California. I wanna live on the beach."

"That's too hot. I want someplace cold. Someplace where there's snow all around. Like a ski resort or something."

"Oh shit," Sarah's eyes widened as she looked in the rearview mirror. Curious, Ana began to turn her head to look behind them and Sarah yelled, "Don't look!"

"What is it?" Ana gasped.

"The sheriff. He's behind us."

Ana's heart rate increased. "Are you speeding?"

"No, not really."

The girls went around a curve in the road and lost sight of him. When the road straightened out, Sarah looked in the rearview mirror and momentarily felt relief at seeing no other cars. But her eyes widened as the sheriff appeared again behind them.

"What happens if we get caught with alcohol?" Ana asked nervously.

"I don't know, but it can't be good," Sarah replied.

Another curve through the small hills approached. When they went around it the sheriff was again lost to their vision. Sarah's eyes darted back and forth between the road in front of them and the rear view mirror.

Once through the turn and on straight road again, Sarah watched the rearview mirror and Ana leaned forward slightly to look in the outside rearview mirror. Both gasped slightly when the sheriff's car appeared sooner than expected. He was gaining on them.

"He's totally trying to catch up to us!" Ana gasped. "Oh, we are so busted!"

"I don't know," Sarah replied calmly. "I might be able to lose him in one of these turns."

"Lose him?"

Sarah simply nodded her head and smiled slightly.

"Oh, gimme a break, your not going to outrun a cop! If he sees you trying to do that we are so dead!"

Another curve in the road approached and Sarah's smile grew.

"Don't!" Ana pleaded. "Seriously! Just drive normally and he'll have no excuse to pull us over!"

"I don't know, this car is pretty low to the ground. I think I could whip around the curve and then pull off on a side road before he can see us."

"Sarah, don't. I don't want to crash and I don't want to get arrested!"

As they started into the turn, Sarah didn't brake as much as Ana would have liked.

"Sarah don't!"

"Oh, alright, take it easy!" she responded as she slowed the car down.

Again they lost sight of the sheriff's car. And again, when the road straightened they watched anxiously in their rearview mirrors. The sheriff appeared even sooner than expected and since the road was now straight, accelerated towards them.

"Crap, he's catching up to us!" Sarah reported.

Quickly the sheriff was within tailgating length of the small Honda. The girls began to resign themselves to being in really big trouble when, from around a curve ahead of them, a pickup truck skidded across the road, tires screeching. It then sped into the straightaway.

Within a second the truck reached the girls and Ana felt as though time slowed down as it passed. She clearly saw two young men in the truck. One was wearing a green baseball hat, smiling slightly as he looked directly in her eyes. The other, the driver, had red, short hair, and his smile changed quickly to a frown when he saw the sheriff's car behind the girls.

The sound of loud rock music blasted its way from the truck's stereo through its open windows and into the open windows of the Honda. Ana recognized the song even though she only heard it for a moment.

Then the truck was past them. The girls both looked in their rearview mirrors and saw the sheriff jam on his breaks, cut hard to his left, and, after making a U turn, turn on the red and blue lights on the top of his car and take off after the truck.

Their eyes wide, both girls looked at each other and smiled.

A few minutes and several curves in the road later, Sarah turned the car off of the concrete and onto a dirt road. Gravel and dust crunched under the tires as they bounced along a fire road.

The girls rolled up their windows as they came around a corner and encountered a cloud of dust. This was evidence that another car had recently traversed the same road. They were getting close.

Ana felt a knot grow in her stomach. Although her unusual good looks drew people to her, she was shy. Other teenagers often mistook that shyness for arrogance and their reckoning for it was swift.

A couple more turns and the girls found their destination: a dried-out meadow between several large oak trees that had become a teenagers' parking lot. Cars were parked sporadically around the field, as were the teenagers themselves. Music blasted from some of the car stereos and mixed together in a cacophonous audio blur.

The girls surveyed the scene quickly and spotted some acquaintances nearby. "There's Stacy and Jenn," reported Sarah, sounding almost relieved. Then she smacked Ana in the arm with the back of her hand. "And there's James!" she cried out, smiling.

Ana retorted, "My God, shut up!"

Sarah parked the car and the girls got out, waving to their acquaintances who were leaning against a pickup truck and holding bottles of beer. As the girls exchanged pleasantries, Ana furtively glanced to her right, checking to see if James was, in fact, there.

In the growing darkness the teenagers' faces became more unrecognizable; but, even at a distance of fifty feet, Ana was able to make out James' handsome countenance. He was chatting with half a dozen or so boys, all with beers in their hands, when, unexpectedly, he turned his head to his right and looked directly at her.

Her stomach tightened as her head snapped back to its original forward position and she pretended to be interested in the seemingly inane conversation going on between the girls. Desperately she tried to use her peripheral vision to monitor James' movements, but the result was her staring roughly in the area of Sarah's chest.

"What are you staring at, lesbo?" Sarah demanded, half jokingly. This snapped Ana from her trance and she stumbled a response, "I'm just spacing out. It's so hot."

Stacy grabbed a beer from a box sitting next to her on the ground and thrust it towards Ana. "Drink a cold beer!"

"Thanks," Ana replied as she took the beer. She knew she had to be cautious. Earlier experiments had proven to her that she was not as capable as her friends in handling alcohol. Only two beers could make her head cloudy and overwhelm her with the desire to take a nap. She took a small sip and tried to concentrate on the girls around her.

James was a magnet. Ana kept reminding herself to not look in his direction. Her head would start to turn to its right seemingly on its own and she would crank it back. Eventually she shifted her position in the group so that James was behind her. Sarah noted this movement, lowered her eyebrows and cocked her head slightly. Ana avoided her gaze.

"How y'all doin?"

Ana spun around, startled by the male voice behind her. Three teenaged boys, all dressed alike in rumpled T shirts, tacoed baseball hats and frayed, baggy jeans, were standing behind her with beer cans in their hands.

Ana turned quickly back around towards her group to see if there was any reaction from her friends. They all just stared at the strangers for a moment before Sarah said, "Hi."

"We just thought we'd come over and say hi. I don't think we go to the same school," the boy in front said with a grin. "Y'all go to Jefferson?"

The girls nodded.

"Yeah, we go to Kingwood. How often y'all come hang out up here? This is pretty cool."

Two of the girls in the group simply looked down, implying that they were clearly not interested. Sarah went the polite route; she humored the boys with a response. Ana could tell by her tone of voice she really wasn't feeling patient about being trapped in conversation with them.

Feigning interest in what the boys had to say, Ana looked over her left shoulder and looked for James. The moment she spotted him he glanced back at her. Her pulse leaped and her head snapped back straight.

"Are you a gymnast?"

The boy next to her had moved in a little closer and was smiling. She frowned and thought for a moment.

"No, why?"

"'Cause you got a real fit body!"

She sighed and looked away.

"What's your name?"

She considered ignoring him, or just using a fake name. But politeness and empathy overrode those considerations and she responded.

"Ana." She said simply, and then looked away.

"I'm Tom!" he said, a little too enthusiastically. She didn't respond. But then felt badly for being rude.

"Nice to meet you," she said apathetically, not looking him in the eye.

"You wanna go for a walk with me?"

"Uh, no, not really."

"Why not, it'll be nice!"

"I like hanging with my friends."

"Aw, come on, come for a walk with me, let's get to know each other."

She sighed, then smiled slightly, "No thanks."

"Oh, are you one of those stuck-up bitches?"

She knew this was a losing situation. She certainly wasn't going to walk off into the woods with this guy, but any negative response she gave to his invitation would be met with aggression and derision.

Again, she sighed, looked down and said quietly, "Nope. I'm not."

"I think maybe you are. What's the fuckin' problem? Oh, are you only into preppie guys or something?"

She just stared ahead, thinking of how to get out of this situation. She looked around the group and each one of her friends was locked into a similarly uncomfortable exchange with one of these new boys.

The boy clearly didn't feel comfortable with her lack of response, so he kept talking.

"So how old are you?"

She gave in, "Sixteen."

"Ah, sweet sixteen! I'm seventeen. You like dating older men?"

She took a sip of her beer and continued to monitor the group, avoiding eye contact with the boy.

"Are you…" the boy's next sentence was interrupted by the sound of another male voice that came from directly behind him.

"Hi Ana."

She turned to find James approaching. Her heartbeat quickened and she was unable to stop a smile from breaking out on her face.

"Hey!" she responded. James noted her smile and returned it.

The boy hassling Ana turned and, immediately after discovering James, frowned.

Ana and James were facing each other with the harassing boy to their side. After smiling at Ana, James turned to the boy and regarded him for a moment too long. Though his face betrayed no emotion, he had sent the boy a signal. Regardless of this, James simply said, "Hi."

The boy stared back at him, also for a moment too long, then simply lifted his chin slightly up and down and said, "Hey."

James looked back at Ana and smiled again. He then turned his head back towards the boy, lowered his eyebrows and said, "You can go now."

The Years Twitch

Ana stifled a laugh. The boy's head and shoulders rose sharply in response to the insult. After thinking for a moment, he muttered, "Pfft," and walked away.

James and Ana smiled at each other but her shyness kept her from keeping his gaze.

"Comeer, I want to show you something," he said as he motioned her away from the group.

They only knew each other because the proximity of their desks in history class. His friends and her friends didn't travel in the same social circles and she knew how much this lessened their chances having a romantic relationship. But she had to admit the quivering she felt in her body when he was near made a mockery of the reasonable part of her mind. It also made her feel as though losing her friends in order to gain a relationship with him would be a worthwhile transaction.

As they walked away from her friends, she felt that quivering overtake her body to such a degree that she became clumsy, slightly losing her footing on the uneven terrain. They had never kissed, but selfishly, unreasonably, she felt that he was already her boyfriend. Nervously she realized that this dark field was the perfect setting for a kiss.

She knew as they walked along that others around them were taking note. This made her feel proud. He was a good-looking boy. And a nice boy. So nice that he seemed rather shy; a fact that worried her slightly about whether or not he'd have the moxie to initiate a first kiss.

Through the darkness they approached a parked car. She could hear him pull keys out of his pocket and her nervousness increased.

"This is my piece of shit," he said, pointing to the car. Because of the darkness she couldn't sort out the make and model, but it looked to be a compact, two-door import.

"It doesn't look so bad," she replied.

"No, but it runs bad," he said while putting a key in the passenger side door. She heard the lock click and he lifted the handle. Pulling the door open caused the light inside the car to turn on and he pointed to the passenger seat.

"Check it out!"

The seat was covered with what looked like carefully laid garbanzo beans. Closer inspection revealed that it was a seat cover made of small beads.

"Ooh," Ana reacted, slightly more enthusiastically than the situation demanded. "What is that?"

"It's a massaging seat cover! Try sitting in it!"

She smiled and got in the car. The tiny beads did, in fact, feel good against her legs and back. She looked at him.

"Wow!"

"I know, right?" he responded and slammed the door shut. After being startled by the sound she frowned. But she was relieved to see him run around the front of the car to the other side and, after reaching the driver's side door, putting in the key and opening it.

He got in, sat down and closed his door. For what seemed like a long moment there was silence. Ana anxiously debated whether or not to break it. There was no denying that she was nervous, and though under normal circumstances she was articulate, currently she simply couldn't think of a thing to say.

He came to her rescue with a comment. "Don't these things feel good?" She simply looked at him and nodded. Even in the darkness she could make out the pale blueness of his eyes and distinguish the details of the long brown bangs of hair that framed his comely face.

"They were actually pretty cheap."

She had difficulty in summoning a response, and as the time for one grew too long, a minor panic started to grow within her.

"Cool," was all she could muster and immediately recoiled at the sound of her own voice. She knew that he was an intelligent guy and for her to use such a pedestrian word must have seemed inadequate to him.

The air inside the car seemed stuffed like hot breath in a balloon. Beads of sweat, summoned by both Ana's temperature and her nerves, formed at the edges of her hairline. She started to strategize a way to wipe her forehead without him noticing when, again, he delivered a small rescue.

"I'm sweating my ass off!" he said with a laugh, and vigorously rolled down his manually operated window.

Relieved, she did the same with hers. The sounds of partying teenagers and cool air rushed in. She took a deep breath. The air seemed sweeter than usual.

"The air smells good out here, doesn't it?" he asked, responding to her deep nasal breath

"Mmmm hmmm," she responded, smiling.

Again silence fell over them. She felt the urge to do something bold, like lean over and kiss him. But she reminded herself that a move like that was typically the guy's job in these situations. The little beads beneath her legs made a clicking noise as she twisted slightly to her left. This opened her body towards him and was the best invitation she could think to give him without seeming too forward.

He glanced down at her mostly bare legs and then jerked his head back up, staring out the front windshield. It was as if he had been caught in an immoral act. Tapping his fingers nervously on the steering wheel, he started to say something but then stopped, apparently thinking better of it.

"What? What were you going to say?" she asked.

He smiled slightly and shook his head. "Nothing."

"No, what were you going to say?"

He turned and smiled at her, laughing a little. "Nothing!"

"What? Tell me!"

His mouth opened just slightly and then he shook his head.

"Don't be a pussy!" she said while laughing. She was simultaneously emboldened by her comment and repelled by it. Shrinking back in her chair just slightly, she awaited his response.

The comment worked. He sat up a little straighter in his chair, turned directly towards her and said, "Will it be awkward in history class on Monday if I kiss you right now?"

She froze. Her body was a tangle of nerves, excitement and muteness. She tried to think of a clever response, one that would be heard in a movie. One part of her brain chastised the other for even trying to come up with anything to say at all. She even considered for a moment if it would, in fact, be awkward on Monday. While all of this was going on James just watched a girl sitting there, thinking, not responding.

"Sorry," he said, looking down.

Her brain numbed.

"No!" she blurted out.

"No? Wait, no what?"

She decided that she needed to give up on words. She leaned forward, grabbed his shirt and pulled him towards her. He smiled and leaned in. In the darkness their mouths missed slightly and she ended up mostly kissing his chin.

He laughed and said, "Are you trying to bite my chin?" Her face turned hot with embarrassment and she felt such a wave of nervousness that she started to tremble slightly. As she again tried to figure out what to do, his hands were on either side of her face. They were dry, gentle and calm. He pulled her to his lips confidently and they kissed.

Unaccustomed as she was to making out in cars, her nervousness quickly transformed to repose and then, as his arms moved from her face to around her waist, sexual arousal.

After a moment she felt an inexplicable desire to touch his ears and did. Her action didn't elicit a negative response from him. This new freedom to touch him seemingly wherever she wanted was exhilarating.

He must have felt the same leeway was being granted to him as he started squeezing her small breasts. She was surprised by how little she enjoyed this. It wasn't that she minded it, she didn't, but she expected that something like this would intensify her arousal. It was clearly turning him on as the intensity of his kissing escalated and he squeezed her harder.

When his lips moved from her mouth to her neck she had to stifle a giggle. Something tickled her. He mistakenly interpreted her convulsive movements as an increase in arousal and thusly his arousal was increased.

But soon she felt more that she was an observer to this entire affair than a participant. She couldn't help but wonder what this was all going to mean later. Were they going to be dating now? What would other people say? Should she care what other people said?

The Years Twitch

She reminded herself of her fortunate position (literally and figuratively) and tried to get back to the moment, but all of these questions in her busy head kept the physical goings on with James from getting the attention they deserved.

Ana didn't notice that he had unbuttoned her shorts and, without warning, he shoved his hand down inside her underwear. His middle finger touching her dry vagina jolted her back to reality like an ice cube being dropped down inside of her shirt.

He knew the cause of this convulsion was not enjoyment and immediately retreated.

"Sorry," he gasped.

"It's ok," she responded nervously.

After pulling his hand back out they both just stared at each other awkwardly.

Then, a little too loudly, he said, "Wanna get a beer?"

Relieved, she responded, "Sure."

The instinctive quickness with which they both responded to their insecurities strengthened their new bond, she thought. But most sixteen-year-olds' senses aren't yet finely attuned. No exception, she had misjudged the situation.

The following Monday morning Ana awoke feeling giddy about the fact that she would see James at school that day. Her mother noted her perkiness and commented on it.

"You seem to be in a good mood today."

Instinctively Ana tried to quell her emotion so as to keep it from Tammy's view. Teenagers often try to assert their independence in such subtle ways and Ana was no exception. She shrugged her shoulders and tried to make her face as deadpan as possible.

Later, the morning ritual of her arrival at school was, on the surface, unremarkable. But Ana looked through the crowd of high-school students for James. When she eventually spotted him about fifty feet away, walking with a couple of other boys, her heart started beating faster. She walked directly toward him.

As she approached him she tried with great difficulty to pretend not to notice him. Out of the corner of her eye however, she was well aware of his exact coordinates.

When the distance between them decreased enough for them to naturally take notice of each another, she allowed herself to look him in the eye. Since he didn't return her glance she waited until she was within a few feet of him, then smiled and said, "Hey."

He continued on his way with his friends, focused on them and didn't seem to notice her. She figured he was engrossed in conversation and simply hadn't seen her.

Presently he was passing close enough that she could reach out and touch him.

"James!" she ventured, this time a little louder than her previous try. This got his attention, but his head turned to face her more slowly than she expected. Other than raising his eyebrows slightly he betrayed no emotion.

"Hey," he said quietly, turned his head back to his friends, and kept walking.

Stepping on, and being bitten by, a hidden rattlesnake on a lonely trail would have brought less surprise and shock to Ana than this humiliation. Despite a surge of emotion, she created an antidote for this venom: she put on a straight face and kept walking as if nothing had happened. Her body tingled and she felt a thickness in her throat, pushing towards her face… pushing tears into her eyes.

While she was trying to figure out why this had just happened, she realized she couldn't be seen in this hallway with tears streaming down her face. Too many people would take notice and want to know what was wrong. The race was on. She had to make her way to the refuge of the girls' bathroom before the water escaped her eyes.

Peripherally she could see some acquaintances of hers standing and talking to her right. She quickened her pace. A rogue tear made its way off of her eye, through her eyelashes and began rolling down her cheek. She slapped it away quickly while lowering her head and hoping not to be noticed.

Once the door to the girls' bathroom came into view, she abandoned her fast walking pace for a run. Another tear had almost freed itself from her eye when she took a deep breath through her nose and widened her eyelids, trying in vain to shake off the emotion that was assaulting her.

Pushing through the door to what should have been the sanctuary of the bathroom only brought another surprise. Two girls were standing by the sinks, looking at themselves in the mirrors and talking. Luckily for her they were so immersed in their own conversation that they hardly noticed her hurried entrance. She got to one of the bathroom stalls as fast as possible, opened the door, got inside and closed and locked the door behind her.

Now the tears were set free. But she couldn't allow for any crying noises as the girls outside the stall would hear them. The teenaged chatting was torturous for Ana. So was her shame. She quickly tried to use reason to abate her emotion, deciding that her reaction was, in fact, an over-reaction. Perhaps in her mind she had built her relationship with James into something that it wasn't; perhaps when she passed him in the hall he was simply locked into a conversation that he didn't want to interrupt.

Either way, there was still a lump in her throat pushing up behind her eyes. As soon as she heard the tittering girls leave the bathroom she allowed herself to cry.

A short time later she found herself sitting at her desk in the first class of the day. She was so distracted she didn't really remember walking there. The teacher went about the daily business of teaching algebra but his monotone voice was hardly noticeable to her. Her next class was going to be history and James would be there. Her stomach started to feel sick with anxiety.

The Years Twitch

A torturous fifty minutes later she found herself floating down the main hallway on her way to history class. The act of appearing normal was much more challenging than she expected. She was the first student to arrive in the classroom and the teacher greeted her robotically. She pulled out her notebook and stared down at it as other students trickled in and sat down at their desks.

The desks were all in rows and James' was next to hers. After a couple of minutes she could sense him walking in and sitting down next to her but she didn't look up. A nervousness shot through her body.

"Hey!" he said in a matter-of-fact tone, but with enough enthusiasm to seem quite normal. She looked up and found him smiling at her. A confused smile broke out on her own face as she cautiously returned the greeting.

"Hey."

He pulled out his notebook and put it on his desk. She didn't know what to do. To her there seemed to to be an uncomfortable silence, but he broke it.

"Did you do the homework?" he asked. She couldn't make heads or tails of what was happening. Maybe everything was normal between them like it had been before this past weekend. Maybe she was overanalyzing everything he did. But their tryst in his car had to have meant something, hadn't it?

"Yeah, I did it," she responded as flatly as possible.

"God, I totally forgot to do it."

The teacher cleared his throat and started the class. Ana found it impossible to concentrate. Her mind was spinning, trying to figure out what was going on in James' head while also trying to figure out what was going on in hers. Shame found its way back into her thoughts.

After fifty interminable minutes the end of class arrived and a jolt of nervousness shot through her body followed immediately by the queasiness of humiliation. She knew that she must be over-reacting to James' lack of reaction, but what he did (or didn't do) when they walked out of class would mean so much to her.

Relief came quickly when he did leave class with her. He made small talk as they walked through the hall together and her mood soared. But she was still uneasy. She knew this emotional rollercoaster was unwarranted, but she was grateful to feel that she was almost through with it.

He reached the doorway to his next class and said, simply, "See you later," while giving her a small smile. She smiled back and replied "Bye." He disappeared into the classroom as she kept walking down the hallway, alone and slightly exhausted.

The next day at school the same pattern repeated. When James and Ana were near each other, but away from their friends, he was charming and articulate. When any of their friends were nearby, however, he didn't acknowledge her presence. It started to dawn on her that he was embarrassed to be seen with her. Once this realization came to her the shame she had previously felt turned to anger.

On her way to school on the fourth day after their make-out session she decided she was going to be cold to

The Years Twitch

him. She felt empowered and justified in her decision to deliver this punishment. How dare he pretend there was nothing between them when their friends were around?

Once she was sitting next to him in history class her resolve was shaken by her attraction to him. Confusing emotion rose within her and she felt an overwhelming desire to wrap her arms around his neck. She must have looked distracted as the teacher decided to break from his lecture and call her name.

"Ana, are you still with us?" he asked, condescendingly. She snapped to attention and responded with a smile, "Yeah!" Her face turned hot with embarrassment as she felt the rest of the class looking at her. Thankfully the teacher quickly resumed his lecture and the attention of the other students was diverted.

The remaining school days of the week found her suffering through the same patterns of hopefulness, shame, attraction and diversion. James began to be predictable, as did Ana's reactions to him. By the end of the school day on Friday she had to concede that he was quite literally controlling her life.

Early Friday evening social preparation overwhelmed the youth of Ana's community. Coming up with something fun to do in a small Texas town was challenging, but they were committed to the task. For teenagers, socializing is taken very seriously, and Ana could feel the weight of the importance of the impending evening on her shoulders. She knew that whatever she and her friends ended up doing, James would likely be there.

Before the sun had set the teen network discovered that a potential victory was at hand. Somebody whose parents were out of town was going to throw a party. Before long half of the student body of the high-school had the address of this party house. Ana's destination was decided.

As the sun sank expectations rose and Ana began the long task of preparing herself for the evening. After showering she was parked in front of the bathroom mirror painstakingly brushing her hair and analyzing her face. Tammy quietly observed the ritual, thankful that the time in her life of obsessing over her own looks had passed. Ana noticed she was being watched and unceremoniously closed the bathroom door. This just made Tammy chuckle.

Ana's goal was to apply her makeup in such a way as not to seem as though she was wearing it. She thought of herself as being expert in this skill, but tonight the distraction of James caused her to overanalyze her work, feel dissatisfied with it, wash her face and then start the process all over again.

She was considering a third attempt when the doorbell rang. Sarah had arrived to pick her up. Anxiety welled within her. After a moment she could hear Sarah exchange pleasantries with Tammy and then heard the sound of her footsteps coming down the hallway. The footsteps grew louder and louder until they stopped outside the bathroom door.

Bam, bam, bam!

Sarah knocked on the door and yelled, "Are you taking a crap in there?"

Ana rolled her eyes and opened the door.

"Hey, what's up?" Sarah said with a smile.

"I don't know, do I look ok?" Ana asked, looking genuinely concerned.

"Gorgeous as usual you fucking bitch! Let's go!"

"No, really, do I have too much make-up on?"

"No, you look great, let's go!"

Ana sighed nervously, took one last look in the mirror and then left the bathroom.

During the drive over to the party Ana tried to maintain casual conversation with Sarah but her anxiety cluttered her mind. That anxiety increased when they pulled up to the suburban house and saw a bunch of teenagers standing on the front lawn. These sorts of social situations were nervous affairs for Ana anyway, but adding James into the equation worsened her condition considerably.

Sarah fearlessly parked her car, yanked the keys out of the ignition, opened her door and while exiting looked back at Ana and said, "Let's go!"

Ana took a deep breath, got out of the car and fell in behind Sarah as they walked towards the house. Some of the kids on the lawn were surprised by Sarah's confidence as she and Ana approached. Sarah would look them directly in the eye and say things like, "Hi, how ya'll doin'?"

Because Sarah was such a strong presence, Ana felt as though she could slip into the party unnoticed. There was something unnerving about the way the other kids looked at her. It was as if their glares had weight and were pushing down on her shoulders.

Slyly she looked for James as they made their way inside. She couldn't see him, but was suddenly accosted by the smell of… her dad's shit?

She crinkled her nose and sniffed. Excitement and bemusement overtook her as she recognized the smell.

Some of her earliest memories were of her father before he'd left home. She had vague memories of lying on his chest while he lay on his bed watching TV. She would try, unsuccessfully, to slow her breathing to his match his.

Sometimes he would lie on the floor and color with her. Other times he would toss her in the air while yelling, "Woo! Woo!"

But the most common memory she had of her father was of him being locked in the bathroom for long periods of time. She would bang on the door, wanting his attention, but he wouldn't let her in. Eventually he would come out and so would the smell.

And Ana was now smelling "that smell" at the party. Her excitement and fear of seeing her father after all of these years was making her shake. Why would he be here? She had no idea where he was, or if he was even alive, so why would he be at a high-school party in suburban Texas?

Following her nose brought her the answer in a flash. She found a group of kids just outside a sliding glass door in the back yard smoking a joint. Ana didn't think that she had ever smelled pot before, but, in fact, she had. Many times. Her dad wasn't going to the bathroom all of those times when she was a kid.

Suddenly many of her old vague memories pulled into focus. Her mother had always talked about what a loser Ana's father was. Here was further proof. When she was a little girl he was locking himself in the bathroom and smoking pot when he was supposed to be taking care of her.

She leaned against a nearby wall and tried to calm down. All of this was too much for her and she started to feel exhausted. Realizing she had lost track of Sarah she scanned the room and saw, through a doorway into a kitchen area, James. Instantly she felt nauseated. This was too much stimulation in too short of an amount of time.

On top of all this she realized she was standing by herself at a party. Embarrassment now entered her emotional equation.

"What's going on?" Sarah's voice was a relief. Ana's embarrassment waned.

"Nothing," Ana said quietly while, despite her effort not to, she glanced quickly at James. Sarah noticed and quickly turned her head to see what she was looking at. After spotting James in the kitchen, Sarah blurted out loudly, "Hi James!" while waving.

"Oh god," Ana whispered to herself as she looked down at the floor. His reaction was unknown to her but she heard nothing.

Sarah turned back to Ana. "Why don't you go talk to him?"

"Shut up!" Ana whispered loudly.

"What? If you like him you should talk to him!"

"Just be quiet, jeez!"

Ana quickly looked towards the kitchen and saw James walking towards them. Not surprisingly she started to feel shaky and looked down at the floor.

"Hey, what's up?" he asked when he reached them. Ana looked him in the eye, replied "Hey," and then looked back down again. A mixture of anger, nervousness, attraction and shame swirled within her.

Small talk between Sarah and James began and it quickly became clear Ana wasn't going to participate. Ana noted an almost imperceptible amount of nervousness in James' voice, and in this felt a small degree of power. In a way she was controlling the situation now. He clearly didn't know what to make of her non-responsive stance and eventually excused himself and walked away.

Sarah glared at her.

"What?" she responded, already knowing what the look meant.

"Why didn't you talk to him?"

"Fuck him."

"I wish you would."

Ana smiled slightly and then walked away from Sarah, through the small crowd, through a sliding glass door and out into the back yard. She stared up at the bright, disinterested stars, wishing their patterns had some sort of code, some sort of meaning that would give her the answers to her questions. But she had to admit she wasn't even sure what her questions were.

"Now what are you going to do? Your engine has quit," John said calmly as he twisted the throttle to idle position. Ana's eyebrows rose slightly as did her pulse. Though the sound of the engine changed dramatically, she instinctively looked at the rpm gauge to confirm that the rotor blades were idling and providing no lift.

Though she knew this was a training exercise, stress caused her muscles to tighten. It wasn't just imagining that this was a real emergency situation; it was also wanting to prove herself to her instructor.

It took a few seconds for her to get the controls set in such a position that the helicopter was gliding down safely. Now she had to find a spot on the ground on which to set it down.

"Where are you going to go Ana? You are running out of time. We are passing through 800 feet."

She surveyed the landscape in front of them. There weren't many options. The best one seemed to be a small parking lot next to what looked like an office building. It was ahead of them and slightly to the right.

"I'm going for that parking lot," she responded quickly.

"Hmmm... are you sure?"

Ana questioned herself but then thought that maybe this was a trick question. She re-examined the lot while trying to keep the helicopter under control, constantly rechecking her gauges.

"Yeah, it looks like a good spot."

"I don't think so. See the poles going around the perimeter of the lot?"

She squinted and then spotted the poles.

"Shit," she whispered.

John smiled and said, "Shit is right. Those are power lines. You fly us into those and we are dead. We are passing through 600 feet. Better figure something out quickly."

Her search began to be frantic.

"Your rpms are dropping, don't stall the helicopter," he warned.

She instinctively pulled back on the cyclic stick and the rotor rpm increased, but she still hadn't found her spot.

"I guess the road next to that building?" she asked, her voice starting to shake.

"Are you asking me or telling me? We are almost down to 400 feet. You better make a decision."

She hoped she was right. "Yes. I'm going for the road."

John didn't say anything and she hoped this was a sign of approval.

They glided closer and closer to the road and Ana began to wonder if they were actually going to go all the way and set down on the pavement.

As they descended to about one hundred feet she heard the engine roar back to life and felt the throttle turning, seemingly on its own, in her left hand.

"I have control," he announced. She let go of the controls and responded, "you have control." His hands and feet were on his set of controls and she sighed with relief at the small break he was allowing her.

As he started flying them up to a safer altitude, he said, "Ok, not bad. There are a few things we should go over, though. Why don't we do that at dinner tonight?"

A jolt of stress rocketed through her already nerve-wracked body. This was not a welcome advance.

"I don't think that would be appropriate," was all she could think to say.

"Why not? It's just dinner! No big deal."

After a short pause she replied, "Can we just concentrate on flying, please?"

"Business before pleasure! Sure I can dig that. Why don't you take the controls again?"

She took all three controls and responded "I have control." This required response sounded rather ironic, she thought. A queasy feeling of weakness fell over her. Trying to sigh through her uncertainty, she banked the helicopter back towards its original course.

"…and then the butterfly valve will be caked with ice, choking off the air from the carburetor. Now you've got a stalled engine. So anytime you lower the collective and get the manifold pressure less than eighteen inches, make sure you pull the carb heat. Even on a hot day!"

As he spoke, John was stared only at Ana. This was distracting as she wondered if he was attracted to her or was being condescending towards her because she was the only female in this helicopter training class. Or both. He was highly recommended as a great pilot and teacher, but she couldn't shake the feeling that he was a creep.

The other four students in the class, all males in their 20's or 30's, didn't seem to notice and appeared to be completely bored by the lecture.

She was surprised by her own earnest interest in the subject matter. She knew that part of her passion was manifested by a desire to prove herself in a world where, rightly or wrongly, she felt unaccepted. Fort Collins,

Colorado was the type of place where feminism could be found running amok, but flight school seemed to be different. She had to concede that her perception of a lack of fairness could solely exist in her head: if she were a guy, her treatment might have been exactly the same.

Thoughts like these were a distraction and she tried to rid herself of them any time they arose.

John wrapped up the lecture: "Make sure you read chapter 26 on 'settling with power' before Friday."

All of the students closed their notebooks and started gathering their belongings. As Ana gathered hers and rose to leave, John said to her, "Hey Ana, comeer for a sec, I want to show you something."

Instantly she was uncomfortable. She looked at the other students and they looked at her and back at John. She imagined them thinking she was getting some sort of preferential treatment from him. Or perhaps she and John had some sort of relationship. The possibility of any of these opinions about her existing in the minds of her fellow classmates made her even more uncomfortable.

She reluctantly responded, "Ok."

He walked out of the lecture room, down a small hallway and through a door into a study room. She kept what she thought was a safe distance from him and when she reached the room, stood outside of it.

He smiled and said, "I don't really have anything to show you, I just wanted to talk privately."

She sighed and looked down, feeling that she knew what was coming.

"I'm really attracted to you and I think we should go out together. We'd have a great time!"

"You're not my type," she responded, probably a little too quickly, or so she thought, and immediately felt guilty for having possibly been rude.

"Or really, what is your type?"

"Jeez you are a pest." Again she thought that she might be too aggressive in her denial. But she was truly getting annoyed.

"Why because I know what I want? That's confidence, darling."

While trying to decide whether to simply walk away or compose another response, she simply stood still and stared at the floor.

He used the silence as an opportunity to keep talking. "Look, I'm twice the man of any of these boys here. Have you ever been with a real man?"

She instantly thought of Jack. Even though she wasn't with him romantically, she felt as though he made her understand what a real man is. Her head nodded slightly.

"Oh, I'm impressed little lady! Well allow me to offer myself as competition for that guy."

She simply shook her head and walked away. Behind her she could hear him utter an angry and disappointed "Pfft!" and then he slammed the door to the study room.

6.

The rotor blades were stalling and her helicopter was falling out of the sky. Ana considered the most plausible reason she had a life flash: she was about to die. Though she had amateurishly yanked on the collective stick in a panicked overreaction, she felt surprisingly calm.

Pulling hard on the collective stick in this type of a situation is like hitting the brakes in a car while driving on ice. She immediately recognized her error and slammed the collective stick down to the floor, hoping to give the rotor blades freedom to spin faster.

The helicopter dropped. Her hope was that in the remaining thirty or so feet of altitude she had left she could gain some speed in the rotor blades, then, just before hitting the ground, pull that collective stick back up again. If the blades had enough inertia, they would cushion her landing at the last moment.

While the stall warning horn blared annoyingly in the cockpit, the trees outside rose around her. They were almost welcoming her, she thought. Details were surprisingly easy for her to discern: the rocks on the ground below, the dust on the bottoms of the trees that lined the road, the small smudges on the windshield… All of these points were seemingly intertwined, collecting themselves around and through her in a way she hadn't known before. There was calmness in her for what surely would have been seen by others as a violent descent.

The Years Twitch

As the rocks, dirt and half-buried tree roots magnified in size in their rapid approach toward her, anxiety rocketed through her nervous system. When she was just a few feet above the ground she pulled up as hard as she could on the collective stick.

The helicopter twisted in a way that surprised her. Instinctively she pushed on her tail rotor pedals to counter the yaw but the helicopter was unresponsive. Instead of landing straight, she was going to hit the road slightly sideways.

Once it slammed into the ground, the helicopter's forward speed caused it to begin to roll over on its side. she pushed the cyclic stick hard to her left to counter the roll but it was of no use. There was no inertia left in the rotor blades.

Even though she was getting thrown violently forward and to her right, she saw the rotor blades hit the ground next to her in an explosion of dirt and rocks. The seatbelt that went over her shoulder held her torso in place, but once the helicopter flipped onto its side her neck snapped so hard that she momentarily lost her vision. All of her senses weren't dulled, though. She could distinctly hear what sounded like rocks in a blender as her ship smashed into the road.

Her seat performed its duty and crushed underneath her, providing a painful shock absorber for her body. Once the helicopter was fully on its side it skidded aggressively forward. The side window and door were now on the ground and were being pushed in. Rocks and dirt launched in through them towards her as if they were being shot from a fire hose.

Fortunately the assault on her face and body by the debris was short lived. She felt the helicopter stop its skid as she tried to breathe, but her breath had been knocked out of her.

Dimly aware that delirium was overtaking her, she felt herself painfully floating. Other pilots, all male, appeared around her, physically holding her breath in their hands. Fighting numbly to retrieve her breath only made the airmen laugh. She had a realization that these were pilots who hadn't survived crashes. Summoning the strength to yell at them, she took a big breath and found herself conscious again in her quiet, mangled helicopter.

Righting her neck brought an avalanche of tiny pains from the top of her head down to the middle of her back. She was dangling awkwardly from her waist and neck. Her seatbelt was still attached to its housing next to her waist. With her right hand she lifted the buckle of the seat belt and was released.

"Uhh," popped out of her mouth as she fell a few inches onto her side. She lay on the broken door and window and pulled her legs away from the tail rotor pedals. A small sense of relief came from being able to move her legs.

After a moment she painfully drew herself to her knees. Draping her arms over the instrument panel, she rested her head on her forearms, taking another moment to catch her breath. The position reminded her of praying in a Catholic church. Though some people become religious after near-death experiences, she noted that she didn't feel changed in that regard.

An eager sleepiness began to overtake her. The strange comfort of her forearms pressing into her forehead was rudely interrupted by a survival mechanism in her brain. She remembered that falling asleep after suffering a concussion could be lethal and it was likely she had one. Trying to break free of the relaxation that was overtaking her body quickly grew into a herculean task, but she was assisted by the thought of...

The radio! It was still lit up, as were the other lights in the control panel, meaning the battery was still working. She found her headset, put it back on and made a Mayday call. There was no response. She tried several more times to no avail.

Outside she noted the tops of the treetops swaying back and forth. The blue sky was now gone, obscured by clouds. Lifting the bottom of the passenger seat, which was now above her, revealed a storage area that contained only one item: her parka. After removing it she slowly put it on, careful to not strain any part of her body that was injured.

She tried the radio again and got no response. The anti-collision and navigation lights were still on and blinking on the outside on the fuselage. After considering turning them off in order to conserve battery power, she decided to leave them on in hopes that another aircraft might pass over and spot her.

Small snowflakes started to gather on the windshield. This was bad not only because cold temperature would make it harder to survive, but also because rescue aircraft might not be able to fly. She had filed a flight plan before she left. She wondered how long it would take before the FAA started checking around to see why she hadn't closed it.

If a rescue plane never appeared, she could simply start walking down the road. It had to lead to a bigger road, if she walked in the right direction. She wasn't particularly comforted by her 50/50 odds. After trying the radio again she pulled out her chart. The fire road she had landed on wasn't represented on it.

Sitting down on the side windshield and leaning against the seat in a fetal position, she watched the silent snowflakes descending in greater numbers. Occasionally hundreds of them would pile up on her round windshield, succumb to their own growing weight and slide off onto the ground.

The silence around her was profound. It was only occasionally broken by the sound of the trees bending slightly in the wind. She could just make out the soft click, click, click of her navigation lights turning on and off.

Ana took a moment to take stock of her own body. Her achy back and neck were painful, but they didn't seem to be seriously injured. Examining different parts of her body after moving clothing out of the way revealed only a few small cuts and bruises, though the ribs on her right side were aching.

Breathing was still a small struggle. She was fairly accustomed to the high elevation of this part of Colorado, so it was possible that she had collapsed a lung. A human can survive just fine on one lung, she knew, but in this altitude it would be hard to keep dizziness at bay.

Suddenly she remembered that she had her mobile phone in her pant leg pocket! Frantically reaching for it caused stinging pains in her back and neck. When she finally removed it from its warm home, the display brought her disappointment. There was no signal. And the battery was at 50%. She had no charger as she had assumed that this was going to be a short trip. Regardless, she thumbed the dial pad on and called 911. There was only a beeping sound: no signal. After trying a couple of more times she sighed and put the phone in her jacket pocket.

Next she tried the radio again and, after receiving no response, put her headset down and went back to staring at the snowfall. Sleepiness began to take hold again and she knew that she needed to fight it. Standing up and shaking it off would be the best course of action, but the position of having her knees being pulled into her chest was keeping her warm. If she just kept her thoughts active she could keep sleep away.

Thinking back on the crash, she was baffled at how she could have remembered twenty-six years of existence in a moment that couldn't have lasted more than a half a second. She considered that time didn't actually exist. It was an illusion created by humans in order to enable our survival in a universe we couldn't possibly be expected to understand. She also considered other important events in her life that hadn't made the cut into the final reel of the life flash. Why weren't they there, had she ended the flash before it's finale, despite its short linear length?

Click. Click. Click. The barely audible sound of the lights blinking on and off were getting further apart. Outside the helicopter she saw a baby duck waddling away with one of the lights strapped to its head. Her first thought was, "how adorable!" But the she realized that she needed that light! She yelled out, "Wait, come back!"

Her eyes popped open and she found herself in darkness inside the helicopter. Confused, she looked outside and could make out pale blue snow on the ground but not much else. Her breath quickened. What was going on? She realized it was nighttime and that she had been asleep!

The good news was that she had survived falling asleep after suffering a concussion. The bad news was that her navigation lights didn't appear to be blinking anymore.

"Shit!" she whispered out loud. She grabbed at the instrument panel, flipping switches in the dark. The helicopter didn't respond. The battery was dead. Knowing it would be futile act, she put on her headset and tried the radio again, but it was dead, too.

There was no way a rescue plane pilot would be able see her now, even if he or she were able to fly. At least the snow seemed to have stopped. She was a bit cold but not suffering. She checked her phone for the time: 10pm.

Her best option was to stay in the helicopter where she was protected from the elements. Once morning came, weather permitting, she could try walking down the fire road or try to make a signal fire. But she mentally took stock of her supplies onboard and there were no matches.

Hunger suddenly announced itself via a grumbling in her gut. Though she was no medical expert, she assumed this was a good sign. There was no food with her, but she knew she could at least stay hydrated by eating snow. When her stomach complained more loudly, she closed her eyes and sent a thought directly to it: "Not now."

She tightened her fetal position and tried to meditate. Light snow began to fall and the quiet, interminable night wore on.

The Years Twitch

Her internal battles, both physical and mental, plus the cruel accommodations of the inside of the smashed helicopter, made for the most uncomfortable night of her life. But dawn did finally arrive, camouflaged by clouds and snow.

Relief at the sun rising mixed with fear, boredom, hunger, pain, claustrophobia, regret, and cold and she was quickly overwhelmed. . She began to shake. Taking deep breaths slowed the convulsions slightly, but it was a chipmunk skittering around outside that brought her respite.

She watched the little creature intently as it zigzagged closer and closer to the front windshield of her helicopter. Surely this must be a sign for her from nature, or God, that everything was going to be ok.

Once the chipmunk reached the windshield it turned its head left and right and its nostrils opened and closed rapidly. Ana smiled and said out loud, "Hi there!" The chipmunk responded by lowering its tail, turning around and dashing off in the direction from which it had approached, a tiny brown blur.

She tried to assign significance to this little event that would make her suffering more bearable. Maybe nature was curious about her, even looking after her. Feeling more motivated she slowly stood up.

Exiting the helicopter was not easy. She had to climb up the seats and out the passenger door (which was now at the top). She then slid down the top of the fuselage onto the snow.

There was about two inches of light powder on the ground. The sky was heavy with clouds but, for the moment, no snow was falling. Another decision was in order: should she wait here and hope the sky cleared enough for a rescue plane to search for her, or start walking down the fire road in hopes of finding civilization? If the weather got bad enough for a plane to be grounded it probably wouldn't be suitable for walking either. Her footwear (boots that were not water proof) would make matters even worse. At least her flight suit and parka would keep her reasonably warm.

With aching shoulders and neck, she walked a few steps up the road to see if she could widen her perspective. The amount of trees made it impossible to get an idea of where the road led. She turned and walked in the other direction about one hundred yards to see if anything worthy of her attention was within view. There wasn't anything, and after checking her phone for a signal (there wasn't one), she turned and walked back to the helicopter.

After sitting down on the main rotor hub and staring across the short bit of road at the trees, she imagined her presence causing uneasiness among them. A slight breeze sent the tops rubbing against each other, creating a subtle whistling sound.

She wondered what to do with herself for a few minutes and then decided to begin the process of meditating. It was always difficult to become a disinterested observer to her own consciousness, but in her current state Ana's challenge was even greater. Because of the slight incline of the fire road, her seat was uneven and she had to use muscles that should have been relaxing to balance herself.

The Years Twitch

Before she could even get slightly into a meditative state, the feeling that she was wasting time overwhelmed her. Bolting upright, she winced at the pain in her back and surveyed the area immediately around her. Near the edge of the road she spotted a rock about a foot in diameter sticking up out of the light dusting of snow.

With a new idea in her head she walked quickly towards it. Though it made the pain in her back worse, she lifted the rock from it's muddy home and carried it to a spot about midway between the side of the road and the helicopter. It made a loud thud when she dropped it to the ground.

After looking around for a moment she spotted another rock just inside the tree line a few yards away. She retrieved it, carried it out to where she had dropped the first one and set it down. The two rocks sat in the short bit of snow on the ground, just touching each other.

Again she looked around for a suitable rock. None was immediately making itself known to her but after a short walk down the road she found a few more. She carried them back, one by one, setting them near the others.

The pattern was starting to emerge. She took a few steps back and surveyed her work. After a moment she decided it needed to be bigger and she went back to work finding, moving and placing rocks.

About twenty minutes later she stood back and checked her work again. This time she was satisfied. From above, the giant arrow comprised of the individual rocks she had put together would be easily visible. It was pointing down the road, to the west, the direction she was going to start walking.

She had to admit that her choice of direction was a guess. The compass in her helicopter was still working and she confirmed by using it that the road she was on was east/west. To walk in the downhill direction would send her west, which was generally the direction she wanted to walk to find civilization. However, this part of the road on which she found herself could be part of a switchback. After walking a long distance she might find the road turning back on itself and heading east.

The odds were really fifty-fifty that she would head in the right direction. But the giant arrow she left for a passing aircraft increased her odds of survival. A rescue team would know which way to head to try to find her.

She stood by the heap of metal and debris that used to be her helicopter and took a deep, pensive breath. A lump grew in her throat. She felt responsible for the death of what seemed like a living creature, and now she had to abandon it. Abruptly she scolded herself for wasting time on this nonsense, turned, and started walking down the path.

The downhill slope made the walk relatively easy. Occasionally the degree of the slope would increase enough that her gait became a shallow run. She was pleased that this pace kept her heart rate high enough that the cold couldn't find its way deep inside her. But a quiet concern starting nipping at her thoughts: would she physically be able to endure this pace for long enough to exit the forest? She was panting heavily.

As her lungs began to tire from the altitude and the exercise, so too, did her pace diminish. Small snowflakes pelted her face. In an attempt to discover the reason she looked up. Was it because it had begun to snow again, or had the wind simply dislodged some snow from the tops of the trees?

She figured that the answer was irrelevant. She needed to keep moving and get off this mountain. Her fast walk became a slow jog.

After about ten minutes of fairly consistent descent, she whispered "Oh no," to herself and quickened her stride. As she came to the bottom of a small downgrade her anxiety rose. In front of her the road turned sharply to the right and out of view. Accelerating to a slow run she followed the path around the curve until it straightened out. She stopped, and then, panting, looked at the slowly rising path ahead of her. Her sense of direction was good enough to know she was now heading in the opposite direction that she sought: east.

"This could just be a switchback," she thought to herself. "But if it isn't, I'm heading up the fucking mountain."

She stood and stared at the road for a moment. It rose up through the trees and turned slightly left out of view.

"Well, standing here like an idiot isn't going to solve your problem. Might as well get moving and see where this leads."

She started jogging up the road. Her hope that it would turn back around to the west wasn't being realized and she started to feel fear gaining on her. The amount of snowflakes that were pelting her face was increasing. She had to admit to herself that it was snowing.

Except for a few short downgrades, the road seemed to be heading consistently upwards. She stopped for a moment to catch her breath and consider her options. She had been travelling for the better part of a half hour. It wasn't too late to turn back and try the other direction. But this road had to lead somewhere… whichever direction she headed. If she was heading up, there was a good chance there was some sort of observation station or ranger station.

After pulling out her phone and checking in vain for a signal she decided to commit to the direction she had been travelling and keep walking. Her breath escaped her even faster now. She thought this was probably because she was gaining altitude, having difficulty breathing or both.

A gust of wind slapped dozens of tiny snowflakes into her face. It felt as though tiny needles were pricking her skin and she had to turn away. She pulled two strings that were on the front of her parka. The hole through which her face peered tightened and became smaller. This provided some relief, but she had to admit that it seemed as though the weather was getting worse.

She increased her pace, but what were previously small pains, particularly those in her right ribs and lung, were becoming more acute. "I'll stop and rest for ten breaths," she thought to herself. With her forward momentum paused, she could hear the snowflakes' clicks as they landed on her parka. The sound of the wind pushing through the trees mixed with the sound of her heartbeat in her ears. It was almost beautiful, she observed, but each sound really could have been a harbinger of her death.

So she kept moving. The snow, the wind, her heart rate, her pain and her fear all increased. "Just keep going," she whispered to herself.

The space between the trees on the side of the road seemed to be increasing. This could mean she was approaching the tree line: an altitude above which trees wouldn't grow. With fewer trees around she thought it might be easier to send a mobile phone signal. But disappointment soon smothered her slight glimmer of hope as she checked her phone. Not only was there no signal, her battery was almost dead.

Suddenly she let out a gasp as someone slapped her in the face. Immediately she turned her head to find that, in fact, there was no one there but that a strong gust of wind had pushed her parka sharply against her cheek. Her hands started to tremble.

The adrenaline shot now coursing through her body got her moving faster. Her breaths were hurried and shaky.

It felt as though with every step, the snow fell harder and the wind blew faster. She watched her feet, feeling as if the entire world was a treadmill spinning below her. Each step she was causing the world to turn and the weather to change.

A sudden gust of wind slammed into her. It felt as if nature was trying to knock her over. "Ha, nice try!" she said out loud as the air whistled through her parka. Her voice had an unusual vibrato and she knew that, despite her previous denial of cold, she was starting to shiver.

Snow was building up on the road. Fortunately it was light powder and not full of water, so her steps were not as labored as they could have been. But each step presented the possibility of a hidden rock, tree root or some other obstacle that could sprain an unsuspecting ankle. Ana cautiously slowed her pace.

Numbness began to take hold of her toes and the stinging in her ribs and lung was getting worse. She assumed her growing lightheadedness was due to the altitude and lack of food, so she tried to ignore it. She was starting to see little spots in her peripheral vision that weren't snowflakes.

Both hers and the mountain's condition remained the same for what seemed like hours. She realized that her stubbornness may have masked itself as intuition or fate and she really should have turned around long ago and walked the opposite way on the road. There was a chance that the road would start descending more steadily soon, but if it didn't she might need to turn around and try to walk back to the helicopter before night fell.

That thought made her queasy with anxiety. Then she remembered her cell phone. Hands shaking from the cold and nervousness, she pulled it out of her parka pocket, but, again, there was no signal. And little battery power left.

The walk continued. Her parka seemed to be stuck to the right side of her face as the wind was consistently coming from that side. The snow she could see in the air ahead of her seemed to be falling horizontally.

The Years Twitch

After about twenty minutes nothing seemed to have changed other than her thighs had started burning. Pulling her hood back and taking a better look around brought her the reason: she had only been walking uphill. There had been no downhill portions to her journey of late. Feelings of defeat started to take over but she reminded herself that even though she was heading up the mountain this road had to lead somewhere. If it led to a simple turnaround she might not survive. If it led to some sort of ranger station or observation station she might be okay.

Her ribs were consistently stinging now. It seemed that the best thing to do was to look down and concentrate on taking one step at a time, more slowly. The snow on the ground was now a few inches thick and each step needed to be carefully considered. The slower pace was easier on her lungs and ribs as well.

Her monotonous steps became rhythmic and she found herself humming a lullaby that her mother used to sing to her when she was a child. Every few bars her voice would quiver as a chill ran through her. She shook off the cold as best she could and kept humming.

Midway through her tenth time humming the song her voice went from a hum to blood curdling scream as she almost walked directly into a large wooden post. While screaming she took three quick steps backwards and then breathlessly yelled "What the fuck?"

In a panic she ripped her hood back off of her head. The post she had nearly walked into was a support beam for a larger structure. On a platform about five feet above the snow was a building of some sort. A fire department observation station or ranger station!

"Ah ha! Ha ha!" she yelled out. "I was right!"

Quickly she found the staircase that ascended to the platform on which the small, square building rested. Battling her desire to race up the steps, she took each snow-covered step slowly and methodically to ensure she didn't fall. Once she made it to the top she found herself underneath the overhang that covered a walkway that seemed to go all the way around the building. Each side of the structure was only about twenty feet long. There appeared to be windows on all sides that were covered with plywood. In the middle of her side of the building was door. Ana ran to it and grabbed the knob, but it was locked.

"Oh for fuck's sake," she said out loud. "Why would you lock this? Who is going to break in?"

She walked all the way around the building to look for another door but found none. After returning to the door she yanked on the knob aggressively in hopes of it being cheap and easily broken. It wasn't, so she stepped back and kicked the door right next to the knob. This sent shock waves of pain through her ribs and ankle. The door didn't respond.

She tried again and again, unsuccessfully. The pain in her ribs and ankle travelled up through her neck and behind her eyeballs. Tears started coming, but she took a deep breath and shook her head in an attempt to hold them back.

She ran her gloved hands over the plywood that covered the windows and found no loose nails or easy ways to pull one of the sheets back to get to the window. Frustrated and shivering, she looked back out at the area around the station and came up with an idea.

After slowly descending back down the steps she walked a dozen paces away from the station. She picked up a rock that was about a foot in diameter and struggled to carry it back up the stairs. After resting it on the balcony guardrail for a moment to catch her breath, she walked over to the door, hoisted the rock to face level and then brought it down on the doorknob. Satisfaction coursed through her veins as the knob gave way. It hung, diagonal to its original position, as if it were unsure whether to fall to the floor or stay attached to the door.

She lifted the rock again, this time above her head, preparing for the final blow, when the door, propelled by a gust of wind, slowly opened a few inches. She laughed out loud and dropped the rock loudly to the wooden floor.

The plywood in front of the windows blocked most light from entering the room, but she could see well enough to make a quick assessment. The building was simply one big room with nothing inside. There was a shelf running around the entire structure under the windows and a small first-aid case attached to the opposite wall. Stepping through the door brought her instant relief from the frigid wind.

For a moment, she didn't know what to do with herself. Then she remembered her phone. She pulled it from her pocket so quickly that her gloved hands lost control of it and it fell to the floor. After hastily picking it up she looked at the display: the symbol for battery power was red but the connection symbol had one bar.

"Oh my god," she whispered. Panic set in as she realized she didn't know whom to call. A tense moment later she remembered 911. She thumbed the numbers in excitedly but carefully and then held the phone to her ear.

There were two static filled rings and then a woman's voice. "911, what's your emergency?"

"Hello! I need help! I was piloting a helicopter over..." Ana was cut off by a chime from her cellphone. Looking at the screen brought her the reason for the sound: there was swirling circle that meant the phone was shutting down. It had no more power.

"No!" she yelled out loud.

Tears started to form again in the corners of her eyes, but this time she let them loose. They streamed down her face as her sobbing began. The convulsing of her body hurt her ribs and she regained her composure within a minute by taking deep breaths. The heavy breathing made her dizzy so she sat down cross-legged on the cold, wooden floor.

Cold, exhaustion and emotion caused her to begin shivering uncontrollably. She unzipped her parka, pulled her legs against her chest and zipped it back up. After laying down in a fetal position on her right side the tears came again.

Again the sobbing was making her ribs ache so she decided she needed to be finished. A few snorts later the tears abated and she simply lay on the cold floor. There was nothing to do but wait, she decided.

A small revelation startled her so surprisingly that her entire body shook. The first aid kit! Forgetting that her legs were trapped inside of her parka she tried to jump up and immediately fell forward on the floor. This caused her to laugh out loud.

The Years Twitch

"Fucking idiot!" she said of herself.

After freeing her legs from the parka she ran to the first aid kit that was attached to the wall, quickly unlocked the handle and opened the small-hinged door, revealing the contents inside. One by one she pulled out bandages, splints and rolls of gauze, only to look at them briefly, say, "no" and toss them onto the ground.

"Oh, come on, there's got to be one in here somewhere, this is the top of a fucking mountain!" she said loudly.

After a few more medical odds and ends were tossed aside, she finally found what she was looking for.

"Yes!" she yelled triumphantly while holding two tightly folded and packaged emergency blankets above her head. She tore the plastic wrapping away and pulled out the blankets. They resembled something that would go in the windshield of a parked car on a sunny day rather than something one would find on a bed. They were reflective silver and had a crunchy texture, but they were designed to retain body heat.

She pulled off her parka, wrapped one of the blankets awkwardly around her torso and then pulled the parka back on. Then she wrapped second blanket around her neck like an awful scarf.

Soon she could feel her body warming the blankets.

After sitting down with her back against the wall she went through the remaining items from the first aid kit. There wasn't much in there of any use other than some Advil.

The constant walking during her journey had kept her blood pumping aggressively. Now that she was sitting, relatively warmly, her heart rate eased. Warmth, relief and fatigue made her feel drowsy. Soon she slept.

When the wind slapped open the station door and startled Ana back into consciousness, she had no idea how long she had been asleep. Cold air rushed in the small room. She stood to close the door and realized it was night as no light was coming into the cabin.

With her ribs and empty stomach grumbling about their painful condition, she decided to descend the steps outside down to the snow. Her mouth was dry and she knew she needed water. Once she reached the ground, she reached down, filled her hand with fluffy white powder, brought up past her lips and then swallowed it down. Immediately she started to shiver so she quickly grabbed a nearby rock, ascended the steps, went back into the station and closed the door behind her. Placing the rock behind the door would keep it closed for the rest of the night, she hoped.

After returning to her original position against the wall she closed her eyes and hoped for sleep. She knew she needed rest and would worry about how she could get rescued when the sun came up. But anxiety was preventing her from getting any rest.

Without warning something skittered across the wood floor just inside of her peripheral vision. She jerked her body erect and snapped her head towards whatever it was, but there was nothing there.

"Oh god, don't tell me I'm losing my mind and starting to hallucinate," she thought to herself.

Again just inside her peripheral vision on the other side of the room something small moved very quickly, but she couldn't turn her head fast enough in order to catch it within her field of vision. Was it a mouse?

"Quack,"

She jumped up and looked around frantically. She had heard a duck quack. There was no way it was a hallucination.

"Quack! Quack!"

It was louder now, and coming from the opposite end of the room.

"Quack!"

She spotted it! It was her old duck, Love, sitting in the corner of the room!

"What the fuck? Love, are you okay, what are you doing here?"

The wind kicked up and shook the boards that covered the windows. Some cold bits of air made it through small cracks in the walls and ceiling and whistled at them. Love started running in circles.

"It's okay," Ana said softly as she bent over and walked slowly towards the duckling. The closer she got the more nervous he appeared to be.

She put out her hands and cautiously moved closer, not wanting to spook the little creature. Love started quacking incessantly, but the sound coming from this little duckling was that of an adult duck, not a baby. Ana's eyebrows furrowed in confusion, but she continued her approach.

"It's okay, baby boy! Comeer!"

The wind kicked up again and the boards of the station groaned and creaked. Love was getting more agitated and as he ran in circles some of his feathers started to fall off.

"Everything's ok baby, I'm gonna take care of you," she said in a high pitched, whispery voice.

The groans and creaks of the walls and the whistling of the wind grew louder and more consistent. Ana lost her balance as one of the boards beneath her cracked and dropped a couple of inches. She regained her balance and took another step toward Love.

Another high volume blast of wind caused one of the boards covering the windows to partially come loose. The glass behind it shattered and snow and wind pushed their way into the small cabin, swirling around. Love was frantic now, jumping up and down and quacking.

"Baby! Baby, it's okay! Let me pick you up!" she implored in full voice.

Another board, this one on the ceiling right above Love, broke lose and was about to fall down. In an instant

The Years Twitch

Ana could see that board was going to crash down on top of Love and crush him.

"No!" she yelled and lifted her foot in order to run and rescue the duckling. When that foot came down it met a weak floorboard. The board cracked and her leg fell through up to her knee. She tried to push herself back up with her other leg, but the board under that leg broke, too. She gasped as a chain reaction began of other boards cracking. More wind and snow blasted through the new openings as if being propelled by some powerful arctic hair dryer.

Love was franticly trying to fly as the boards beneath him cracked and popped. Before the board above him finally crashed down Ana looked up to see the rest of ceiling giving way, snow and debris falling from above like some sort of macabre prelude to her death. She tried to push herself up with her arms, but the floorboards beneath her hands gave way and she fell onto her torso. Legs and arms dangling below her, she looked through the hole where the floorboards had been and saw nothing but clouds. The boards beneath her torso began to groan under the strain of supporting her and finally gave way.

As she fell into the abyss, the sound of the smashing timber diminished behind her. Though she knew she was going to die, she was calm enough to realize that her life had not flashed before her eyes again. Did her life only flash before her eyes if she was going to live?

Her gut felt queasy as she fell. This made no sense, she thought, why was she falling? But there was nothing to do, she had no control.

From below a wallop of wind pushed up against her, blasting her hair from her face and causing ripples in the skin of her cheeks. She felt like one of those skydivers she'd seen on TV: arms and legs spread wide and seeming to fly.

The air from below was so powerful that after a moment she was sure that she was floating and not falling. Somehow she knew that she was safe. And she knew instinctively that Love was safe as well. As she tried to turn herself around to look for the duck, she felt herself losing control and starting to fall rather than float. So she let go of trying to find him and regained control.

In the distance around her grey streaks of clouds circled around her like she was inside a tornado. The clouds were moving horizontally, yet the strong wind was still blasting up from beneath her. Again, this made no sense to her, but she just stayed calm and observed.

She found herself in the middle of a cloud cylinder that started to spin faster in a pulsing fashion. It was as if she were in some giant washing machine. The cloud walls began to make a noise like the washing machine her mother used when Ana was a child. Womp. Womp. Womp. Womp.

Her heart started pumping furiously when the walls started spinning faster around her. The corresponding sound did as well. The cadence of the washing machine became that of a helicopter. Every wallop of sound was followed so quickly by the next that there was never any silence. And the walls started closing in.

Calming herself by taking a deep breath, she watched the walls spinning faster. The whirling sound grew louder and her blood pressure increased.

The Years Twitch

"They are only clouds, they can't hurt me," she thought to herself. But the cyclone spun even faster, the walls moving so fast that they were a blur. And they tightened closer around her floating body.

She couldn't stop the panic that was swelling within her. The wall of clouds around her kept constricting to the point that she could almost reach out and touch it. The noise was deafening.

Finally the wall contracted enough to grab her outstretched arms and legs. She screamed as she was violently thrown to her side.

Her scream awoke her from her dream. In a confused instant she found herself still in the ranger station, her back against the wall and her legs stretched out on the floor in front of her. But she had lost her balance and was falling to her left towards the floor.

Putting her hand down stop her fall, she gasped as she tried to shake the numbing effects of sleep away. The loud whirling sound from the cyclone was still loudly audible and her trembling body and mind couldn't discern reality from dream.

It only took about two seconds for her to realize that this was, in fact, not a dream. And the loud whirling sound was that of a very real helicopter outside!

"Oh my god!" she screamed as she jumped up from the wall. She took two steps towards the door but her exhausted heart could not get blood to her head fast enough and everything in her vision turned white. She fell forward and down onto the floor, face first. The impact was so great that she broke her nose and the pain brought her back to consciousness.

Groaning as she got to her hands and knees, she watched blood drip from her nose down to the floorboards. The pain in her mind and her body was excruciating and overwhelming. But the loud sound of the helicopter outside was a startling motivation and she again jumped to her feet.

This time she kept her head low as she ran to the door. Once she reached it she grabbed the broken handle and pulled, but the door wouldn't budge. The rock she had put in its path blocked the way.

"Fuck!" she yelled, bending over and picking up the rock. She threw it unceremoniously into the room and flung the door open. Searing white sunlight blasted her eyes and temporarily blinded her. It was as if someone was standing on the front porch with a spotlight. She put her hand in front of her eyes and ventured outside.

Unable to look up for the moment, she looked down at the stairs and the bright white snow on the ground below. Apparently daytime had come and sunshine with it.

The sound of the helicopter began to diminish. Quelling panic, she ran down the stairs as quickly as she dared. Once at the bottom she ran out into the ankle deep snow waving her hands in the air. Her eyes had adjusted to the sunlight enough that she searched the sky for the helicopter. She could still hear it, but not see it.

Turning around she spotted the tail of the helicopter disappearing behind the tree line. The loud noise of the

The Years Twitch

rotors became muffled and she held back the urge to scream.

She had to do something, and do it quickly. There was no flare gun in the first aid kit back in the station, but there were matches. While sprinting back up the stairs she saw her own blood on the snow and wood.

The door had gently closed itself and she threw it open violently. She dashed across the room to the first aid kit and tore through its contents until she found the matches. The sound of the helicopter grew quieter.

She ran as fast as she could back across the floor, out the door, down the stairs and then stopped. Panting, she looked at the protruding corner of the walkway of the station. "That'll do."

Shaking, she removed three matches from the box and lit them all at once. She held the small flame they created against the wood of the edge of the walkway.

"I'm sorry for doing this, but I have to burn you down," she said to the station. She felt that the station would understand. A signal fire had to be lit in order for her to be found.

The wet wood would not cooperate. The flame of the matches burned down until it reached her fingers and she had to drop them. Tears started to form in her eyes as her shaking hands produced another three matches from the box. She lit them and held them against the wood. The sound of the helicopter was now distant.

"Come on, come on."

The wood of the station would not comply. Again she dropped the burning matches once they reached her fingers. Again she lit three more. Holding them against the wood summoned some steam into the air but little else.

"Please for fuck's sake, please! I don't know why I didn't think of this sooner," she desperately whispered. A tear fell down her face while a drop of blood fell from her nose onto her upper lip. She wiped them both away and tried to concentrate on the matches through the immense pain in her face.

Another three burnt-out matches fell to the snow and another three were lit. She could now see some small fibers at the end of the log started to smolder. There was no helicopter sound now.

"Come on, come on," she coaxed out loud. A tiny red ember appeared where she had been holding the flame. In the back of her mind she was aware that the helicopter was gone, but if she could get this place burning someone would hopefully notice the smoke. But she was also burning down her shelter.

More burning matches were put against the wood and the tiny ember grew to be two tiny embers. She watched as the flame on her matches moved closer and closer to her fingers. She wanted to keep the flame against the wood just a little longer. Another tear dropped from her eye and rolled down her cheek.

"Whap bap bap bap bap bap!" The loud wallops of a helicopter arose behind her. She spun around to find a Eurocopter Astar helicopter floating up from the valley below.

The Years Twitch

Waving her hands frantically, she screamed and stepped out into the field next to the station. She could clearly see a male pilot and observer in the helicopter and they both waved.

The pilot slowly moved the helicopter toward her and once over the small field, gently set it down. She was smiling so hard her face hurt.

The observer in the passenger seat opened the door, stepped out, and ran over to her.

"Are you Ana?" he yelled over the sound of the helicopter's engine and spinning rotor blades.

"Yes! Yes, I'm Ana!"

"Are you hurt?"

"I'm ok! Actually I think I have some broken ribs, but I'm ok!"

"What about your nose?"

"Oh, yeah, that's probably broken, too!"

"Ok, come on, let's get out of here."

He took her by the arm and walked her to the running helicopter. The desire to collapse into him and let him carry her was overwhelming but she fought it until they reached the back door of the chopper. After getting into the back seat, she leaned back and took a big, painful breath. The observer ran around the front of helicopter to the opposite back door and got in. Seatbelts and headsets were put on Ana and himself and then he said, "Ok John, we're ready to go." The pilot in the front put his left thumb up in the air and then sped up the rotor blades. The observer opened up a first aid kit, pulled out some gauze and cotton and started cleaning Ana's face. She started to tremble.

"It's ok, you're safe now," the observer said calmly while smiling slightly. The helicopter slowly floated away from the ground.

She nodded but started to shake even more. Tears pushed against her eyes and she couldn't hold them back. Soon she was sobbing and her body began to convulse.

The startled observer leaned back to give her room. But she leaned into him and put out an arm like a child wanting its mother's love. Immediately the observer understood and put his arms around her. Their awkward embrace caused the right half of his headset to be pushed from his ear onto his nose. He pulled away from her and when she saw what had happened they both laughed.

After being released he said, "You're a lucky girl."

"How did you find me?" she asked through sniffles.

"Well, we had your flight plan, but it was the cell call you made that gave us a track."

"Are you serious, that worked?"

"Yep."

"I can't believe that."

"Gotta love technology."

"Where are you taking me?"

"Mercy Hospital."

After looking out the window and watching their descent for a moment, her gut seized up.

"Pilot!" she called out in a slight panic.

The pilot turned his head. His aviator sunglasses hid his eyes, but she could tell he was looking at her.

"Make sure you've got your carb heat on!"

The pilot laughed and said, "Don't worry, we're safe!"

She laughed a little and realized she was probably being irrational.

After a moment the pilot asked over the headsets, "Young lady, I have a question for you."

"Yeah?" she answered.

He turned his head back so he was facing her and lowered his sunglasses. She could now see his eyes, and recognized them! It was John, her old instructor!

She gasped and smiled. John then said, "Now will you go out with me?"

7.

A commercial plane flight shouldn't be more painful than being captured by the Taliban! William was trying to find comfort in a cramped aisle seat. His flight home from Afghanistan should have been an occasion to rest, but flight attendants and other passengers kept banging into his elbow as they walked up and down the narrow aisle.

This was the final leg of his journey. Originating in New York, this flight would stop in Denver, then fly to Los Angeles. He knew that once he was there he would have to battle traffic, but then he would finally be home to see his worried mother.

John pulled his SUV to the curb of the departure terminal at Denver International. Ana smiled at him and reached for the door handle.

"Wait," John blurted out. "No kiss?"

Ana had to confess to herself that instinctually she didn't want to kiss him. She wasn't totally sure why she had been dating him for the last two weeks, but she had a lot of guesses. His being older than she was might have been one of the reasons because she never really knew her dad.

And John was confident. Possibly too confident. "Pushy" might be a better word to describe him. She knew that she simultaneously feared men's power because it could be used to hurt her but also feared living without that power close by because it could be used to protect her.

In a way she felt that John had earned her concession. But was her guilt reason enough to date him?

This trip to the Robinson facility in Torrence, California for a safety seminar might be the perfect break to reassess their situation.

She smiled, said, "I'm late," leaned over and kissed him on the cheek, then grabbed her bag, closed the truck door behind her and jogged into the airport.

"Did you fall off of your skateboard?" asked the elderly lady sitting in the window seat to William's left. The middle seat between them was empty. The lady pointed at the cast on his arm.

He smiled and thought for a moment. The idea of telling this woman his entire story seemed overwhelming. He simply shrugged and said, "Something like that."

The lady kept his gaze in a way that made him slightly uncomfortable. After a moment she blurted out, "Do you know why prostitutes are called hookers?"

He couldn't help but laugh slightly as his eyebrows rose in surprise.

"No, actually I don't!"

"Well, in the civil war there was a certain Union major general who enjoyed drink, ladies and losing to the south!"

He smiled, suddenly interested in where this was going. But his concentration was broken when he noticed a pretty young woman coming down the aisle from the front of the plane.

He looked back at the older woman and she continued.

"This general set up shop around the corner from the White House, believe it or not, and would have all night parties in which young ladies were in attendance."

Ana made her way down the aisle of the airplane, feeling sweat building up on her forehead. She carried her bag in front of her with her right hand. It was heavy and probably a little too big to be a carry-on, but she didn't want to check it. With her left hand she looked at her ticket: 26B. A center seat. She hated center seats.

As she passed the other seated passengers and looked above them at their seat numbers, she made a quick calculation about where she would be sitting. It looked as if there was a good-looking young man in an aisle seat next to an empty center seat. She felt a pang of embarrassment when she admitted to herself that she was a little bit excited by the idea of sitting next to a handsome guy.

Out of the corner of his eye William noticed Ana approaching. He found himself hoping she'd be sitting next to him and then feeling stupid for having had the thought.

The elderly lady continued, "Late at night, or early in the morning, the ladies could be seen leaving this general's house…"

She stopped talking and looked up. "Hi sweetie."

Ana was standing next to William in the aisle and pointed at the empty middle seat.

"Is that 26B?"

"I think so," he responded, and began taking off his seatbelt.

"Thanks," she said as she lifted her bag up into the overhead compartment.

William rose and stepped into the aisle to make room for her to get to her seat. She slid through and sat down. He returned to his seat and as he was re-buckling his seat belt, the elderly lady blurted out, "The general's name was Joseph Hooker!"

He laughed and said, "That's really interesting!"

Ana smiled and looked back and forth between the two. William smiled and shrugged his shoulders. She felt as though there was a clear opening here for her to join the conversation that was already in progress. She pointed to the cast on his wrist.

"War injury?" she asked jokingly with a smile.

The smile on his face was immediately gone as he looked at his wrist. "Ya," he said quietly.

Her smile disappeared as well. What had she done? "God Ana, you are such an idiot. The guy has a crew cut and is wearing fatigues, did you ever think that maybe he actually got the injury while on duty?" she thought to herself. She desperately tried to think of something to say to change the subject as her face and ears starting heating up with embarrassment.

"Dude, you are such a dick. She's trying to have a conversation with you. Speak!" William admonished himself in his mind.

Both sat awkwardly for a moment.

The elderly lady suddenly said, "Who wants a mint?" Ana and William both looked to their left and the lady held open a small metal box with white candies inside.

Both Ana and William smiled and accepted the mints.

Another short, uncomfortable silence ensued, and then Ana felt confident enough to break it.

"See this black eye?" she said to William, pointing at her right eye. He looked at her.

"I actually hadn't noticed it," he replied.

She smiled.

"You are sweet. I got it crashing a helicopter."

"Are you serious?"

"Yep."

The plane's intercom system crackled as one of the flight attendants began robotically reciting safety procedures, interrupting Ana and William's conversation.

The engines whined to life and within minutes the plane was bouncing down the taxiway. Both Ana and William wanted to continue their conversation but the interruptions wouldn't cease. Eventually the captain announced that they were going to take off without delay and that the flight attendants should take their seats.

While staring forward William considered his luck. He was sitting next to someone who was attractive enough to make his nerves rattle.

Was this chance handsomely disguised as fate?

The plane thundered down the runway and soon its bouncing tires were floating in the air. The landing gear retracted into the belly of the plane as they all rose. After a few moments of flying due south at one eight zero degrees, the captain turned the plane west towards two seven zero.

The Years Twitch